"JE VOUDRAIS UN BAISER.
'I WOULD LIKE A KISS.'"
TESS GIGGLED.

"Would you?" Alain asked.

"Would I what?"

"Would you like a kiss?"

"Of course not, silly." She giggled again. "I'm conjugating verbs, remember?" She took a sip of her tea.

But as she put her glass back on the table, Alain took her forcefully in his arms and started kissing her.

It was crazy, but nice, too. In spite of herself, Tess felt herself kissing him back. But Dave's image would not leave her mind. . . .

Bantam Books by Suzanne Rand
Ask your bookseller for the books you have
  missed

Winners Miniseries

Sweet Dreams Romances

WINNERS

THE GOOD LUCK GIRL

Suzanne Rand

BANTAM BOOKS
TORONTO · NEW YORK · LONDON · SYDNEY · AUCKLAND

RL 6, Il age 12 and up

THE GOOD LUCK GIRL
A Bantam Book / May 1986

Midvale's answer to perpetual motion, this friendly cheerleader can usually be found with Dave Prentice or the rest of the cheering squad when she's not cracking the French books . . . Tess hopes for an international business career . . . So diet-conscious that she's got everyone calling tossed salads "Tessburgers," Tess admits she worries too much. She shouldn't, because the rest of the school expects our good luck girl to get everything her heart desires!

Entry under Tess Belding's picture in *Midvale Memories,* the high-school yearbook

ONE

"I want to propose a toast," Tess Belding announced to the two other girls who sat cross-legged on her bedroom floor. She raised her glass of ginger ale. "To the best friends a girl ever had! You've both been lifesavers. I'd have been lost without the two of you helping me move all this stuff." She gestured toward the cartons that surrounded them and the piles of clothing strewn across both the stripped twin beds. "Be sure to tell your father how much I appreciate his letting you use the station wagon, Gina."

"He didn't mind," Gina Damone assured her. "Especially not when I volunteered to take Mama grocery shopping this afternoon so he could stay home and watch some science show on TV." She looked at her wristwatch and groaned. "How can it be four o'clock already? I told Mama I'd pick her up at a quarter after, but I hate to leave you in the lurch, Tess."

"I've got to go, too," Stacy Harcourt said, rising from the floor so gracefully that Tess wondered, as she often did, why she hadn't been born willowy and beautiful like her best friend. "But Jeremy and I can come by tonight to help you put things away if you want," Stacy continued.

"Please, don't worry about it. You've both done more than enough already," Tess insisted, struggling to her feet as Gina jumped up in one swift, athletic movement. "Anyhow, I told Dave I couldn't go out tonight, so I'll have plenty of time to straighten up tonight and tomorrow."

"What are you and your mom going to do for Easter dinner tomorrow?" Gina asked. "Is your dad taking you somewhere?"

"Are you kidding? I think he felt like he had to be a good sport and offer to help us with the moving. But that definitely cured his guilty conscience. As soon as he and Mom get back and unload the last load, he'll be in that rental truck and out of here. I think Mom and I are going to have a quiet meal here together tomorrow."

"You really think he just helped out because of guilt?" Stacy asked, looking sad.

"No, not really," Tess admitted. "But partly. I mean, I know he doesn't hate Mom or anything like that, and he still loves me, but whenever he's around, I can tell he feels sort of like a rat by the way he talks fast and won't look either of us in the eye. I know Mom wanted the divorce as much as he did. But I think he feels like a traitor for heading out west. I can tell he's excited about the idea of living in California, but he doesn't want to show it." She shrugged.

"He's definitely moving?" A shadow of sympathy clouded Gina's luminous brown eyes.

"Oh, he's definitely going, all right. He's even got his plane ticket. I think it's great he's finally doing what he always wanted," Tess insisted brightly. "I know I'll miss him, but my place is with Mom. She says she doesn't know what she'd do if she didn't have me to help her."

"You two should be fine here," Stacy said, glancing around Tess's new bedroom. "Everything's nice and new."

"And cramped," Tess added. The townhouse at Clover Farms Estates had looked enormous when her mother had first taken her to see it. But now that the rooms had furniture in them, they all looked tiny—especially Tess's bedroom. Even the windows had been better in her old home: her bedroom there had had windows on two walls, so that the sun lit it brightly all day long. With just a single narrow window, her new room grew dark by early afternoon.

"Your room's as big as my bedroom," Gina reminded her. "And the bathroom is great. Your old house didn't have a built-in vanity complete with makeup lights and drawers."

"Yeah, it's not so bad," Tess said, walking with Stacy and Gina out of the bedroom and down the short flight of carpeted stairs that led to the living room. "Mom says we couldn't have done better for the price. I guess it's just going to take me a while to get used to it."

"I'll definitely be using the pool in the summer," Gina promised.

"I can't wait to check out the tennis courts," Stacy added. "It will be such a relief not to have all those creeps at the country club watching me and showing off their backhands."

"Like Dex Grantham?" Gina asked impishly as the two of them filed out the front door.

"You went out with him more times than I did," Stacy retorted.

Tess waved from the doorway as her friends walked toward the parking lot, laughing and teasing each other. She was smiling as she closed the door, wondering what Dex would say if he knew his old girlfriends laughed about him. Of course, it was easy for Stacy and Gina to laugh about Dex, because they were both involved with other guys now. They wouldn't think it was so funny if they were talking about breaking up with Jeremy or Tony. Tess couldn't even imagine losing her own boyfriend, Dave. A shiver ran up her spine as she turned toward the stairs.

Then she laughed at her silliness. A lot of things in her life had been unstable recently, but, so far, her relationship with Dave Prentice wasn't one of them. In the seven months they had been together Tess and Dave had been known as one of Midvale High's most solid senior couples.

Tess had been astounded the first time Dave

asked her out. She'd been in awe of Dave Prentice ever since they'd met in the ninth grade. He'd struck her as aloof in spite of his popularity. He was a quiet standout as both an athlete and a student. In the freshman English class they'd shared, Dave had never taken over the class with long speeches like some of the straight-A students, but he'd always known the right answers when called upon. Dave was tall and fair with a shy smile and penetrating gray eyes, someone Tess had thought of as a serious guy. And she'd assumed that anyone so serious might regard a talkative girl like her as shallow.

But when they were together, Dave brought out the more serious and introspective part of Tess's nature, and Tess's outgoing personality coaxed forth the extrovert within Dave. They'd struck a perfect balance, and Tess eventually dismissed her qualms and accepted Dave's love for her.

Tess went upstairs, hoping to avoid her parents when they returned with the final load from the old house. She wasn't comfortable seeing them together. She'd known about her parents' breakup for months—as soon as they'd told her, her father had moved into an apartment. But the divorce had become final only two weeks ago. It was still too soon for Tess to know how to act when she was with both of them. She was nervous just watching how formal they were with each other. The divorce had made all the Beldings more polite than they'd ever been when they were one family.

As she entered her new bedroom, Tess flicked on the overhead light. The weak glow barely affected the gloom of the approaching twilight. She stood in the doorway, almost overwhelmed by the clutter. Clothes needed to be hung in the closet. Cartons of books had to be arranged on the shelves that lined either side of the narrow window. Two little lamps had to be found and unpacked to lighten the gloom. The *Cats* poster and Midvale pennants should warm the place up once they were hung.

As she surveyed the clutter, Tess realized how much of her old room she had managed to bring with her. Once everything was in place, the new room wouldn't look so small and cold. Clover Farms Estates was one of the nicest townhouse communities in Midvale, after all, and there was absolutely no reason why Tess shouldn't be happy there.

"Tess Belding, this is the first day of the rest of your life," she announced out loud, her cheerful voice echoing off the bare walls. "You're Midvale High's good luck girl! Everything's going to be terrific."

But as the echo reverberated in her ears, Tess's face fell. She knew that the first carton she ought to unpack was the one that held her French books. Spring break was nearly over, and it was time to get cracking. Why had fate chosen to make her life so hard?

TWO

"Un moment, s'il vous plâit." Mr. Calhoun held up one hand to stop the students who had jumped out of their seats the moment the bell announced the end of French class. He continued in English, "Please stop at my desk to pick up your last quizzes on the way out."

Tess yawned as she rose from behind the long table in the language lab. It was only Monday afternoon, but Tess felt as if she'd been in French class alone for an entire week. Her arms and legs ached and her eyelids were drooping. She had unpacked boxes in her bedroom until late Saturday night, then spent most of Easter Sunday unpacking kitchen boxes and arranging furniture.

She snapped to attention when she plucked her graded quiz from the scattered papers on Mr. Calhoun's desk. A big D was scrawled at the top. "Oh, no, not another D!" she moaned.

"I'm afraid so, Tess," she heard Mr. Calhoun say. "Do you have a few seconds before rushing off?"

"Uh, sure, Mr. Calhoun," she agreed, even though she knew Dave would be waiting by her locker. Except for French and English, all her classes were in the vo-tech wing, so she and Dave rarely passed each other during the day. Even their lunch periods were different. But Dave would have to wait, after a D in French.

Mr. Calhoun rose, and Tess followed him to the windows, swallowing hard to ease the lump in her throat.

"You don't look pleased with your grade," he began.

"Of course I'm not pleased!" She tried to control her voice, but it cracked from nervousness. "How could I be?"

"I'm sorry, Tess. I didn't mean to sound sarcastic. Believe me, I wish you were doing better. I know it's important to you. I also know you were getting C's and even some B's last year, which makes me wonder if there's something in my teaching methods that's putting you off."

"Oh, no, Mr. Calhoun! It's not you, honest," Tess said quickly. "I was really glad when I found out I'd be taking French with you this year. It's just—" She started to shrug, then felt another yawn coming on.

"Staying out late when you've got school the next morning?" he asked, with a hint of disapproval.

"No, I never stay out late on school nights. I'm not totally irresponsible, you know," Tess replied with spirit. She shook her head in misery and stared out the window at the playing field

8

below. "I'm sorry. I guess I must *seem* pretty irresponsible, getting two D's in a row on quizzes. But I really don't stay out all night. I just had a long weekend. My mom and I moved to a condo, and I was unpacking and putting junk away until late."

"You and your mother moved over the spring break?"

She nodded, but his question seemed to demand more of an explanation. "My folks just got divorced and sold our house. So Mom and I moved to a townhouse out in Clover Farms Estates. I made sure I unpacked my French books first," she added, trying to lighten the tone of the conversation.

Mr. Calhoun smiled. "That's the spirit!" he said. "I don't mean to come down on you, Tess—I hope you know that. I'm aware that you work extra hard, and I'm sure this must be a difficult time for you. I hadn't realized your folks split up, and I've moved once or twice myself, so I know that's disorienting. I'd just hate for you to get a D on the midterm. It wouldn't look good on your records."

"I know that." She heaved a deep sigh, trying to relax. "I've got about six weeks yet, right? I promise I'll crack down, starting now." She waved her quiz paper. "I'll learn these irregular verbs if it's the last thing I do."

"Atta girl!" He clapped her on the shoulder. "Let's see how this week's quiz goes. If you're still having trouble, maybe I can get you some extra help. Better run now. I don't want to make you late for your next class."

"Thanks, Mr. Calhoun. I really am going to do better." Stuffing her quiz paper into her folder, Tess hurried out the door and down the stairs to the ground floor. She was too late to meet Dave at her locker, but she had to pick up her steno pad, anyway.

She was pleasantly surprised to spot Dave leaning against her locker when she arrived.

"Where've you been?" he asked impatiently. "I was just scribbling a note to tell you I'd split. I can't be late for algebra."

"I'm sorry." Tess stood on her toes to plant a kiss on his cheek. "Calhoun wanted to talk to me after class," she explained, tossing her French text into her locker and grabbing her steno pad. She slammed the door shut and quickly twirled the combination lock.

"Anything wrong?" Dave asked, the impatience in his voice replaced by concern.

"Let's put it this way," she said dryly, hooking one arm through his. "Nothing's especially right. I just got another D on a quiz, and Mr. Calhoun's worried I'm not going to get my act together before the midterm." She turned to walk toward the tunnel to the vo-tech wing.

"That bad, huh?" They started walking faster, almost trotting, as the first bell rang. As Tess released Dave's arm to turn down the tunnel to steno class, the bell drowned out Dave's words.

"I can't hear you!" she shouted.

Dave had reached the doorway to his math class by the time the bell stopped, so his words echoed through the hall. "I said I know you'll do fine. There's no way you'd let yourself get a D in any subject. Especially when it means suspension from the cheering squad for your last semester of school." He smiled as he backed into class. "Meet you before baseball practice, okay?"

Tess tried to race down the chilly cinderblock tunnel, but her legs suddenly felt like tree trunks. Kicked off the cheering squad! She hadn't thought of that. Dave was right. A single midterm D meant academic probation for the rest of the semester, and academic probation meant no cheerleading. Her misery would be complete if she got a D in French and lost her position on the cheerleading squad.

Tess actually liked French. She longed to live in Paris one day and had been looking forward to high school as much to start studying French as for any other reason. Mrs. McCready, her business typing I teacher, had had a seminar on careers; when she'd spoken about the career of bilingual secretary, it had seemed like a job created for Tess.

But after three and a half years of studying French, Tess still confused verb tenses, still had trouble remembering which nouns were feminine and which were masculine, still turned idioms into malaprops. As she slid into her seat in stenography class and flipped open her steno pad, she flushed at the memory of the faux pas she'd made in French class just the week before.

11

Mr. Calhoun had played records by two French singers, then asked Tess which singer she preferred. Tess meant to say, "It's all the same to me." But instead of *Ça m'est égal*, she'd blurted, *"C'est moi-même."* Not until she heard everyone chuckling did she realize that she had actually said, "It's myself"!

Tess's pencil raced across the pale green surface of the paper as Ms. Arnold, the teacher, began to dictate. But her usually swift fingers fumbled as her thoughts returned to French. When the class members exchanged steno pads to correct them, Marilee Swietzer gaze Tess an odd look as Ms. Arnold reread the dictation. Tess knew the exercise hadn't been up to her usual high standards.

Sighing in exasperation, Tess flipped the pages to begin the second exercise. She smiled grimly as she held the pencil poised, ready for Ms. Arnold's first words. She expected to struggle in French class. As much as she loved the language, it was never going to come easily to her. But typing and stenography had seemed like second nature to Tess. If she began to slip in her vo-tech courses, she couldn't expect anything else to go right.

THREE

Beginning Monday after school, Tess tried to throw herself completely into her studies, but the harder she thought about concentrating, the more difficult concentration became. Worries about grades and cheerleading crowded her mind. And getting used to Clover Farms Estates was as hard as she'd expected.

Tess wasn't used to facing an empty house after school. Her mother had taken a full-time position at The Bookworks, the big bookstore at the mall. She worked until six P.M.—until nine on Thursdays—so Tess was on her own until at least 6:30 every evening.

Tess also had more chores in the townhouse. She had always cleaned her own room and helped with the dinner dishes, but her new duties included starting dinner, tidying whatever mess she and her mother had created that morning in the bathroom, and stacking the breakfast dishes in the dishwasher.

It had seemed like a challenge at first. Before

moving Tess had planned a series of exotic dinner menus. "I think we should do a Chinese night," she had suggested enthusiastically, her nose buried in a cookbook titled *Wok Magic*.

"That would be neat," her mother had agreed. "What were you thinking of making?"

"Oh, I don't know," Tess had answered blithely. She'd skimmed the index. "Maybe hot-and-sour soup and dumplings and beef with snow peas."

So far, Tess hadn't tried any of those recipes. By the time she got home from school, she couldn't face all that measuring and mixing and chopping. Instead, she stuck to heating dishes her mother had prepared at night. A meatloaf shared by two people lasted a long time, Tess discovered. The most complicated meal she prepared that week involved breading two fish filets and slicing some vegetables for a salad. Tess's plans for exotic cuisine had quickly dwindled to a menu as exciting as school lunches.

Stacy invited Tess and Dave, Gina and Tony, and Jeremy to eat dinner at her house on Friday and watch a movie on the VCR. Tess was thrilled, especially when Stacy told her that Emma, the Harcourts' housekeeper, had offered to prepare one of her specialties. Tess was already addicted to Emma's brownies and cookies.

Tess tried to study on Friday afternoon. But her attention wandered, even though she didn't have to worry about cooking. As she read her

French assignment—a short story about a young woman's arrival in Paris from her country home—Tess found herself caught up in the tale and ignoring irregular verb forms. Soon she stopped reading altogether and began day-dreaming. She had left Clover Farms Estates behind for a day in Paris, where she was surrounded by the bustle of the busy streets, the smell of freshly baked *baguettes*, the sight of workmen on their bicycles and chic women in the latest fashions. The fantasy was a delicious escape from verbs, tests, chores, and grade averages, but when she next looked at her watch, half an hour had passed.

Somehow, Tess managed to police herself diligently enough to wade through the entire story and scrawl answers to the questions in her workbook. But by then it was past six, time for her mother to arrive and for Tess to dress for dinner. She still had three pages in the text to translate, but she could save those for over the weekend.

As she stacked her books on top of her desk, Tess heard her mother's voice calling, "Hi, Tess, anyone call for me?"

"No, Mom." Tess went downstairs, where her mother was hanging up her coat in the little closet at the back of the living room. "How was work?"

"Exhausting!" Beth Belding looked tired, but she was smiling as she sank onto the couch. "I got spoiled working part-time, I suppose.

15

And wearing jeans, too. I don't think I'll ever like wearing panty hose and heels," she admitted, kicking off a navy pump. "Maybe I just wasn't meant to be dignified and respectable."

"You *look* respectable," Tess assured her. "I don't know if you look like yourself, but you look respectable."

"If I don't look like myself, who do I look like?" Her mother laughed as Tess perched on the arm of the chair across from her. "I know what you mean, though," she added, reaching to remove the bobby pins from her hair. "I think I'll wear my hair down from now on. I wasted half the day trying to stick these pins back in. Now that you put that henna on it, I don't look so much like a gray-haired hippie, do I?"

"You always look good, Mom." Tess was surprised. Her mother actually sounded concerned about her looks. "When you let your hair down, you don't look much older than I am. I wasn't crazy about it up."

Mrs. Belding yawned. "I feel ten times better with those shoes off and that ton of lead out of my head." She bent over and shook her hair into fullness. "Fifteen minutes with my feet up and then a long bubble bath, and I may even feel human again."

"At least you don't have to work tomorrow," Tess reminded her cheerfully.

"Mmmm." Her mother closed her eyes and leaned her head back. "I should be thankful for small favors, huh?"

"Let me get you a drink," Tess offered, jumping up. "Then I'll hurry in and out of the shower so you can take your bath.

"Here, Mom." She came back from the kitchen with two glasses of apple juice.

"Thanks, Tess, you're an angel." As her mother leaned into the lamplight to take the glass, Tess noticed the lines of weariness around her eyes.

"I didn't start anything for dinner, since Dave's picking me up to go over to Stacy's. But if you want, I'll be glad to fix something for you."

"Thanks, honey. You really are a big help, you know?" She raised her glass to her lips, then leaned back again. "Mmmm, that tastes good. . . . Don't worry about me," she said lightly. "I'm going out for dinner myself. No pots or pans to wash tonight!"

"Where are you going?" Tess was curious. Her mother hadn't made social plans in months, not since her father had moved out.

"One of the men who comes into the shop now and then asked me to have dinner with him. At Casa Mia, no less." She raised her eyebrows as she named the expensive Spanish restaurant.

"A dinner there probably goes for what we spend in a whole week on groceries! Maybe you can get lots of doggie bags," Tess teased. "Then you won't have to eat my cooking next week." Her mother didn't answer. When Tess looked over, she seemed to have dozed off. Tess headed for the stairs.

It's really nice that someone's taking Mom out for a decent meal, Tess decided as she rushed in and out of the shower. *Still*, she thought, blowing her hair dry, *Mom should have mentioned it earlier*.

Tess had expected her mother to date, but she hadn't imagined that it would happen so quickly. Patricia Petersen's mom had gone to singles bars and mixers when the Petersens first split up. *But that's not the same as having a date*, Tess told herself as she applied the white under-base she used to keep her rather ruddy skin fashionably pale. As she sponged on her foundation and added blusher a thought struck her, and she hurried downstairs to wake her mother.

"The bathroom's all yours, Mom," she said gently to the form stretched out on the couch.

Mrs. Belding rose with a start, rubbing her eyes. "Don't tell me I dozed off!" she said in alarm. Then she looked at her wristwatch and relaxed again. "Well, I guess I needed a quick rest. I've still got plenty of time to get ready. How come you're done so fast?"

"I can do my eyes in my room after I get dressed," Tess explained. She hesitated, then asked the question that had occurred to her upstairs. "Mom, this guy who's taking you to dinner—he's not married, is he?"

"Don't tell me you're planning to keep tabs on your own mother!" Mrs. Belding laughed, but Tess didn't smile in return, and her mother's voice grew serious. "You don't have to worry about me, honey. One married man was enough in my life, and that one was married to *me*. No, Burt's a widower."

"Oh." Tess shifted her weight from one bare foot to the other, not knowing exactly what to say. Now that she'd interrogated her mother, she felt foolish. What right did she have to tell her mom whom she could see for dinner? "I'd better hurry," she finally said, bolting for the stairs. "You know how Dave hates to wait."

Tess couldn't help smiling in relief as she tugged on her tan jeans and searched in the jumble of her closet shelf for her oatmeal cotton sweater. A widower! He was probably sixty years old and lonely, just the sort her kind-hearted mother would feel sorry for. She'd probably be stuck looking at photographs of all his grandchildren through the entire dinner.

Her mother had come upstairs while Tess was dressing. Tess made up her eyes carefully, smudging on overlapping shades of crayon and then applying mascara in bright blue to offset the neutral colors of her outfit. As she left her bedroom, she could hear singing over the noise of the shower.

She stopped outside the bathroom door for a minute to listen. She didn't recognize the tune—like Tess, Mrs. Belding was usually off-key—but the singing was definitely a good sign.

Tess tapped on the door, then stuck her head into the steam-filled room. "I'm going downstairs now, Mom!" she called through the misted glass of the shower door. "Dave should be here any minute."

"Will you be at Stacy's all night?" her mother shouted back.

"I think so. I'll be home by midnight. Don't bother waiting up for me if you don't want to."

"Okay, dear, have a good time. Oh, Tess, do you think I look better in my green silk dress or the black knit outfit, the one with the beading and the scooped-neck top?"

"I like you in both," she answered. "I guess I'd wear the black. It's dressier, and Casa Mia's supposed to be a pretty fancy place."

"I think you're right," her mother called, then began to sing again.

Smiling, Tess hurried down the stairs and took her royal blue bomber jacket from the closet. Her mother was obviously excited about going to Casa Mia. It was the sort of restaurant Tess's father had always insisted was too expensive for anything but a business meal.

Tess heard Dave's signature knock at the door—one loud, two soft—and hurried to open it. She couldn't blame her mother for being excited. Tess herself was thrilled at the idea of eating anything she hadn't put in the oven herself.

FOUR

"Anyone for seconds?" the Harcourts' plump gray-haired housekeeper asked the six teenagers seated around the oak plank table in the enormous kitchen.

"Mmmm, I think I'll take you up on that," Dave answered, scooping up the last forkful of mashed potatoes on his plate.

"Me, too," Tony Genovese chimed in. "Your potatoes are the best, Emma."

"Just a chop for me," Jeremy added. "No potatoes or corn, thanks."

"It's nice to see you boys really tuck in," Emma said as she took the empty platter and bowls to the sink. "Stacy here doesn't eat enough to keep a bird alive."

"That's not true, Emma!" Stacy protested, rising to clear some plates from the table. "It's just that once in a while a little self-control comes in handy."

"When you're a cheerleader, you've got to

watch your weight," Tess added, although she was dying for another helping of potatoes.

"You all look pretty good to me," Dave said, his eyes taking in Stacy and Gina but lingering on Tess. Tess flushed with pleasure. When her friends complained that their boyfriends rarely noticed the pains they took with their hair or clothing, Tess couldn't join them. Dave frequently told her how good she looked.

"Speaking of self-control," Jeremy said, his green eyes crinkling in amusement, "I can't stand the suspense another minute, Stacy. What movie did you get for the VCR?"

"I didn't get one," Stacy answered smartly, pirouetting away from the table with another load for the dishwasher. She laughed at the disappointed looks that followed her announcement. "Only because I finally got around to making a list of what we've already got. I figured we could come up with one everyone wanted to see."

"I'll vote for a Clint Eastwood," Dave piped up.

"No violence, please," Tess groaned. "Let's see a comedy—Woody Allen or something."

"Anything's fine with me," Gina said easily.

"Don't talk like that!" Stacy warned her, returning to her seat and pulling a folded piece of paper from her pocket. "You know how guys are: if these three decide they're dying to see *The Texas Chainsaw Massacre*, we'll have to wrestle it away from them."

Gina laughed. "Come on, Stacy! I can't picture your parents buying that one to add to their collection."

"Well, they don't have that one. But they've got one or two real dogs. Here's the list," she added, spreading it out in front of her. "I left off all the bad ones and the ones I've seen too many times to sit through again."

"I'll be going upstairs before you kids start arguing," Emma told them, hanging her apron on a hook near the stove. "Just because my apartment's on the third floor, don't think I can't hear you if you start acting up. And I'll be down to check on you, too." She smiled. "There's plenty of soda in the little refrigerator in the den, Stacy, and there's ice cream in the freezer. I think we've got rocky road, peanut butter cup, and butter brickle."

"Mmmm, rocky road!" Tess murmured.

"Tess! Don't forget, spring practice starts next week," Stacy cautioned.

"That's right," Dave teased. "When you're a cheerleader, you've got to watch your weight," he said, mimicking Tess's speech at dinner. Even Tess had to laugh at his perfect imitation.

Jeremy had gotten to his feet and was reading the list of movies over Stacy's shoulder. "What about *Rocky*?" he asked. "I never got to see that."

"Why don't we each write down the name of the movie we'd like to see the most and draw straws or something?" Tess suggested. "That seems fair."

"Not if I don't get to see *Raiders of the Lost Ark*," Tony protested. "I've been dying to see that another time."

"I wouldn't mind seeing that again, either," Jeremy put in.

"Me either," Tess and Gina said at almost the same time.

"What do you say, Dave?" Stacy asked. "Should we put in our votes and let them see it?"

"Sure, why not? I'd rather go with the flow than have to start pulling names out of a hat."

"Okay, that's settled then." Stacy got to her feet with a sigh of relief. "Let's go put that one on before everybody changes their minds."

It was close to midnight when Dave turned into the drive leading to Clover Farms Estates. He pulled into the parking lot and switched off the ignition.

"Have a good time?" he asked softly.

"Great," Tess answered, leaning toward him as he reached out for her.

For a minute or so, neither of them spoke. Tess closed her eyes and absorbed the softness of Dave's lips, the warmth of his skin, and his sweet, masculine scent. Finally, she murmured, "There's just one thing I'd have changed."

"What's that?" Dave whispered, nuzzling her neck.

."We should have left earlier, so we'd have more time here," Tess said, raising her lips to meet Dave's again. Finally, regretfully, she pulled away. "I'm almost late."

"Don't want that to happen," he said, kissing her again. "C'mon. I'll walk you to the door." He reached around to open the car door.

Tess reached for Dave's hand and squeezed it gently as they walked up the path. She was surprised to see the front of the townhouse ablaze with lights. Her mother was always talking about having to economize these days. Tess would have to remind her to leave on just the outside light when she went to bed.

Dave stopped Tess just before they reached the glare of the house lights. "This will be my first good-night kiss to you at your new house," he said, pulling her closer. Tess smiled as his soft lips met hers once again.

"But not the last, I hope," Tess said as they parted.

"Definitely not the last," Dave said. Then, with one more quick kiss to her cheek, he turned back toward the parking lot and disappeared into the darkness.

Tess was surprised to hear soft music through the closed front door as she put her key in the lock. Her mother rarely stayed up past ten these days. She was even more surprised when she walked in and saw not only her mother but a man—sitting close together on the couch, holding hands!

"Oh, hi, Tess, I didn't realize it was so late!" Her mother's voice was high and unnatural, and her face was flushed with color. With a start, Tess realized she had interrupted her mother in the middle of a kiss. She was speechless and just stood staring at her mother and the stranger. A flush of anger and embarrassment burned her face. Mothers weren't supposed to have make-out sessions on the living room couch. The whole thing was ridiculous.

She still hadn't found her voice when Mrs. Belding said, "Honey, this is Burt Holland. Burt waited until you came home because he's so eager to meet you."

Tess looked hard at the man who was rising and extending a hand to shake. He certainly was not old and doddering. This man was tall and broad-shouldered, and there wasn't a speck of gray in his hair.

Tess offered her hand, which felt small and frail in his big, warm grasp. "I've really been looking forward to meeting you," he told her, a little gap between his front teeth making him look even younger when he smiled. "Your mother talks about you all the time."

"Nice to meet you," Tess mumbled. *All the time?* He made it sound as if her mother were his lifelong friend.

"Burt's invited us for dinner at his house next weekend," her mother said, rushing to fill the awkward pause that had followed the introductions. "He's been telling me he's a gourmet cook, and Chinese is his speciality! When he found out you were crazy for moo shu pork and sweet-and-sour shrimp, he insisted he cook for us."

"Great," Tess said flatly. She shoved both hands into her jacket pockets. She wanted only to escape to her room. She clenched and unclenched her fists inside the pockets and fought the shiver building within her. Her mother and Burt were staring at her, waiting for her to speak. "That should be nice," she added, trying to sound enthusiastic.

Burt sat down again. He started to drape one arm over her mother's shoulders, then suddenly pulled back and folded his hands in his lap. "My son's going to be thrilled," he said pleasantly. "Having one of the Midvale cheerleaders to dinner in his own house!"

"Oh, does he go to Midvale?" she asked weakly.

"He's a junior this year. You might not know him very well, though. Paul doesn't go out for a lot of athletics. He's more the studious type, you might say."

"Oh, sure, I know Paul." Tess forced her lips to curve into a smile, then, tugging off her jacket, walked on stiff legs to the closet and hung it up. "I'd better get to bed now. It was nice meeting you, Mr. Holland. 'Night, Mom."

As soon as she'd turned onto the staircase, her smile faded. Paul Holland's father! That was too much. Only a parent blinded by loyalty could have described Paul as "more the studious type." *More a complete social zero*, Tess told herself as she took the steps two at a time. Paul Holland told bad jokes, laughed loudly at his own humor, and looked as if he dressed in the dark.

In her bedroom, Tess put on an old Van Halen album to drown out the sound of Mr. Holland's voice and her mother's laughter and flung herself across her bed. In their old house, Tess never had been able to hear noise from the living room in her bedroom, even though all the rooms were on the same floor. Well, not till Mom and Dad started arguing, she admitted to herself. Still, the new house seemed too small for decent living.

Tess felt more trapped than ever within the narrow confines of her room. Her old room may not have compared to Stacy's sprawling, perfectly decorated quarters, but this new one seemed like a cruel imitation of the real thing.

She switched off the stereo and stomped into the bathroom to wash her face and brush her teeth, hoping the sound of her heels on the floor would remind her mother that someone in the house wanted to sleep. When she'd walked back down the short hall to her room, she shut her door as loudly as possible without actually slamming it.

After she had changed into the old football jersey of Dave's she'd begun wearing as a nightgown and had flicked off the light, Tess noticed that things had quieted down on the first floor. But she hadn't heard the front door open and close. Burt Holland hadn't left. Tess squeezed her eyes closed to fight the mental picture of her mother and Burt on the couch, necking like a couple of high-school kids.

In bed, she tossed and turned for what seemed like hours, feeling the pulse throbbing in her temples, relaxing only when she finally heard the front door being closed and locked and her mother's muffled footsteps on the stairs.

Tess really didn't expect her mother never to look at another man. The divorce was final. But her mother had wasted no time becoming thoroughly involved with someone—someone who was Paul Holland's father! The prospect of her mother and Burt Holland in a serious relationship was torturous to her, but she couldn't push the thought out of her mind. Like a mosquito bite, it kept demanding her attention.

If her mother married Burt Holland, Tess would be Paul Holland's stepsister. She couldn't bear to stand in the same cafeteria line as Paul Holland, much less sit across from him at the dinner table.

My brother the nerd, Tess told herself, kicking off the covers in frustration. But when she realized how carried away she had become over her mother's first date, she giggled aloud.

Paul wasn't really that bad—as long as he wasn't related to Tess Belding. Paul Holland was a show-off, always demanding the spotlight with wisecracks and practical jokes. Sometimes he was even a little bit funny, but he didn't know when to back off. Tess considered herself the patient sort, but Paul Holland was like a gnat on a warm summer's night. He buzzed and buzzed and buzzed until even a saint would have wanted to swat him.

Her muscles aching with fatigue, Tess tried to concentrate on something pleasant. She had too much to do the next day to spend the night tossing and turning, especially over a nonexistent problem. Lots of people had a couple of dates and never saw each other again. Surely her mother wouldn't tie herself to one man so soon after her divorce.

Look on the bright side, Tess told herself. *Forget about Mr. Holland. Forget about the chance you'll flunk French. Forget about not getting into the right secretarial school and about getting suspended from the cheering squad. Forget about how cramped this townhouse is, how the walls are thin as paper.*

The cheeriest subject Tess could think of was Dave. When Dave wrapped his arms around her, Tess's cares slipped away. His kisses wiped out the rest of the world.

Remembering the gentle caress of Dave's lips on hers finally did the trick. Tess snuggled deeper into her pillow as sleep overcame her. As long as she had Dave, everything would turn out all right.

FIVE

I guess things are going to get worse before they get better, Tess thought when Mr. Calhoun handed back the latest French quiz on the following Tuesday. The note at the top of Tess's paper said, "Please see me after class." It was right next to her grade, a C. Tess thought that showed *some* improvement. Unfortunately, it wasn't enough of an improvement to guarantee the passing midterm grade she needed to avoid academic probation.

"Bye-bye, cheering squad," she muttered under the cover of the clanging bell.

Mr. Calhoun looked at her with disappointment when she approached his desk. "What happened, Tess?" he asked gently. "I thought you were really going to crack the books for this quiz."

"Oh, I know—and I did my best, honest I did!" she insisted, her voice trembling. "But the last few weeks have been crazy—packing, getting moved into our new house, spring cheering practice. I'm not trying to make excuses, but sometimes I just can't concentrate!"

"Maybe what you need is some outside help," the teacher suggested.

"You mean like private French lessons?" Tess shook her head. "We couldn't afford that right now."

"Whoa! Don't jump the gun on me, Tess!" Mr. Calhoun smiled. "I didn't say anything about paying for private lessons. Here's what I was thinking. Last summer when I was in Paris, I struck up a friendship with a family named Blanc. Well, their teenaged son Alain had always wanted to visit the States, and he'll be arriving this weekend to attend Midvale as an exchange student. He'll be staying with my wife and me, and I'm sure he won't mind tutoring you. In exchange you can clue him in on what's what in Midvale. He'll be a senior here, even though he'll still have a year of specialized study to complete at the *lycée* when he returns home."

"Tutoring me? You mean after school and at night and stuff like that?"

"Stuff like that." Mr. Calhoun nodded. "What do you think?"

Tess thought that she would rather jump off a rooftop to find out if she could fly. But at the moment she would have taken Russian lessons to stay in Mr. Calhoun's good graces.

"It doesn't seem fair to him," she said doubtfully. "I mean, his idea of seeing America probably doesn't include sitting around with a dodo who's flunking out in his native language."

"Well, we'll have to leave that up to him," Mr. Calhoun said. "But Alain's a nice guy, and I'm sure he won't mind. After all, what boy wouldn't rather be with a pretty cheerleader than an old married couple? Let's see what Alain says when he gets here. We're picking him up at the airport on Saturday."

"Okay," Tess agreed feebly. "And thanks a lot for trying to help, Mr. Calhoun."

"You look down," Dave said when she got to her locker, where he was waiting. "Blow the French quiz?"

She shrugged. "I got a C−. It could be worse. But now Mr. Calhoun's gotten this bright idea to have some exchange student tutor me. That means I'll be even more hassled for time than I already am!" She switched books, then slammed her locker closed.

"Look on the bright side." Dave grinned impishly. "He'll probably be tall, dark, and handsome and fall madly in love with you. Then you'll throw me over and run off with him to 'Gay Paree' while I stay here and die of a broken heart."

Tess snorted with laughter. "What've you been doing, watching the late show? I'm sure he's a wimp. Wonder how you say that in French?" she mused as they started walking down the hall. Dave's arm encircled her shoulders, and she leaned against him, thinking how strong and solid he was. *"Un type pathétique?"*

"What's that mean?"

"A pathetic guy," she translated. "And I'll bet he is. I mean, even his name's boring. Alain Blanc. Do you know what that is in English? Alan White!" She giggled. "How's that for a romantic name?"

"He's probably suave and mysterious," Dave teased. "Maybe his name's dull, but one look at him and you'll decide I'm just a hulky hick."

"Or a hicky hulk." Tess giggled. Then she gazed up at Dave solemnly. "The thing is, I haven't got much choice. If I flunk French, it's goodbye to cheerleading. And probably goodbye to studying at Winston, too. I'm sure they're just dying to accept a student in their bilingual program who's failing her second language!"

"Second? What's your first?"

"Very funny," she told him dryly. "Maybe you should get a job writing material for Johnny Carson."

"Hey, come on, take it easy!" He pulled her more tightly against him as they stopped at the corridor where they usually separated. "I know things have been rotten for you lately, but you've got to keep your sense of humor. You're Tess Belding, remember? Always on top of everything."

"Yeah, that's me, all right. The awesome Tess Belding, the girl who's got all the luck."

Shocked at the bitterness in her voice, Tess forced a smile. "At least I've got you," she whispered, reaching up with one hand to tousle Dave's sandy hair. "I don't know why you put up with me sometimes, Dave."

"Because I love you, that's why," he answered softly. He leaned down to plant a quick kiss on her lips, then straightened up. "Besides, you kind of grow on a guy. You know, like moss."

"I suppose you're crazy about me just because I put up with your terrible jokes. Look, I'd better run."

"Meet me after practice later?" he asked.

She shook her head. "I can't, not today. I've still got this morning's dirty dishes to clear before I start dinner—and my bedroom's a disaster area. You'd think a little place would be easier to keep neat. And if I don't put in at least an hour on verb conjugations, I'll never pass the next quiz. But call me tonight, okay?"

"Okay," Dave agreed as she hurried away. He looked so disappointed she was almost tempted to say she'd see him at Nicola's after practice. But he was out of sight by the time she changed her mind.

Steno and word processing were too demanding to allow Tess to think of anything else. By the time she was hurrying to the girls' locker room to change for cheering practice, she'd forgotten her depression and was whistling

"On, Mighty Mustangs," the Midvale fight song, between her teeth.

Her good mood lasted while she changed out of her khaki jumpsuit and flats into shorts, a T-shirt, and sneakers, the squad's usual spring practice gear. Practices were still being held in the gym, but Tess was in the mood for sunshine and baseball.

"You sound full of team spirit!" Gina said cheerfully, dumping her purse on the bench between the lockers just as Tess was tying her sneaker laces. "Let's hope our mighty Mustangs show the same kind of spirit at next week's baseball game."

"I didn't even realize I was whistling," Tess admitted. "Was I off-key again?" She laughed ruefully. "I definitely have no reason to be in a good mood. We got another quiz back in French. My grades are still the pits."

"If I can help you study, let me know," Gina offered. "Between the Italian I get at home and the Spanish I get here, I ought to be worth something."

"Oh, don't worry," Tess assured her. "Mr. Calhoun's already called in reinforcements. He's found some French exchange student who's starting school here next week."

"Did I hear someone say those magic words, 'exchange student'?" Stacy asked as she languidly opened her locker and started changing clothes. "I thought we weren't having any of them this year."

"I guess we are, after all," Tess told her. "I don't think this one's exactly official. He's the son of a friend of Mr. Calhoun's."

"A French guy in our class?" Stacy's blue eyes sparkled. "*Oooh la la!* I can't wait! Remember Erik, that gorgeous Danish guy in tenth grade? He looked just like Bjorn Borg! What a hunk!"

Tess shook her head sadly. "The poor girl will never be normal," she told Gina with feigned concern. "Do you remember the fabulous Erik? The only thing he had in common with Bjorn Borg was a Scandinavian accent. Really, Stacy, he was the worst! Those short pants! That awful crew cut! I swear the guy never cracked a smile."

"Well, maybe he wasn't really gorgeous," Stacy admitted. "And he *was* pretty boring on our one date. But all foreign men are glamorous in a way, don't you think?"

"My father and brother will be thrilled to hear that," Gina joked. Her parents had emigrated from Italy seven years before, when she was ten.

"Your brother doesn't count," Stacy retorted. "Dino's just nine—he's as American as apple pie. But I think your father's pretty glamorous. I mean, he's not at all like American men."

"No," Gina agreed, laughing, "he wears suspenders and sings opera loudly."

They all laughed with her. Tess was pleased

to hear Gina speak fondly of her father. Not long before, Gina had seemed almost ashamed of her parents, but she'd come to appreciate them more in the past year. Dating Tony, who was proud of his own Italian heritage, had helped.

As the girls laughed, the juniors on the squad—Patricia Petersen, Kathy Phillips, and Sherri Callahan—arrived.

"What's so funny?" asked Sherri, a pretty, boisterous redhead. "Has Paul Holland been through here?"

Tess's good mood abruptly deserted her. She busied herself hanging up her jumpsuit as the other girls continued to chatter.

Sherri shook her deep auburn curls. "He had me in tears at lunch today. A ten-minute routine on spring sports—baseball, soccer, and competitive sun-tanning."

"How can you be so friendly with that little nerd, anyhow?" Stacy asked, making a face.

"Paul? Oh, he's not that bad." Sherri shrugged. "He's really bright, you know, and he's actually pretty funny—except for his jokes, that is."

"He's kind of sweet when you get to know him," Kathy agreed.

Of course, Kathy thinks everyone is sweet, Tess thought. The shy, pretty girl never spoke unkindly of anyone.

"Maybe so," Stacy relented. "But he's just so frantic all the time. He makes me nervous."

"C'mon, Stacy, nothing makes you nervous,

and you know it!" Tess had meant to tease her friend fondly. But her voice had an unfamiliar cutting edge.

"What's with you?" Stacy asked. "Or did you just get out of bed on the wrong side today?"

"It's impossible to get out on the wrong side of my bed," Tess cracked. "The room's too small!" But her humor failed again, and suddenly all the girls were giving her the same look Stacy had. "Don't mind me," she muttered. "I guess I'm just worried about my grades and peeved because I can't go to Nicola's after practice."

"Not going to Nicola's?" Patricia's eyes widened in her pixie face. "That's a first for Tess Belding!"

Tess shrugged. "I just can't hang out after practice all the time now that Mom's working," she said.

Gina walked over and put her arm around Tess's shoulders. "Tess," she began, "we're your friends. Remember that if you need some help—with anything."

"I'm sorry," Tess said. "I shouldn't take any of this out on you guys. I'm really sorry I snapped at you, Stacy."

"Is having practice twice a week too much for you, Tess?" Stacy asked. Her tone was kind, but Tess felt a shiver go up her spine nonetheless.

"Oh, no, Stace! Practice is one of the few

things I look forward to. Even if it meant staying up all night, I'd never quit the squad! I've just got to get my French grades up or I'll be on academic probation. Then I'll have no choice."

"Probation!" Sherri gasped. "You mean there's really a chance you'll be kicked off the squad?"

"Of course not," Gina said staunchly, one arm encircling Tess's waist in a hug of support. "Tess is no dummy. Just wait," she said to Tess. "Soon you'll be getting A's in that class!"

"And you'll have fun doing it, too," Stacy said slyly, "now that you've got this Frenchman to help you study."

"Who?" Patricia squealed.

"You mean you guys haven't heard about the new man in Tess's life?" Stacy asked, winking at Tess.

As they headed to the gym Stacy told the juniors about the mysterious Frenchman who would soon be Tess's personal tutor.

"At least I have a little bit of good news for you," Gina told Tess as the two lagged behind. "Stacy and I decided that we'll definitely be doing just one new cheer this season. And absolutely no double splits!"

"That's the best thing I've heard in ages!" Tess exclaimed, remembering the complicated split routine that had been so hard for her during football season. "Maybe my luck is changing."

"You can make it change, Tess," Gina said

firmly. "That's one thing I learned during the winter when I was so miserable over Dex Grantham. Only you can make yourself happy."

"I know you're right, Gina. And I'm trying, believe me." But there wasn't much she could do about her mother and Burt Holland, or meatloaf dinners, or Clover Farms Estates, or the hours of tutoring with some French nerd that stretched before her.

SIX

"Where to next?" Dave asked as he and Tess left the Midvale Quad Cinema on Saturday night. "Want to stop in at Nicola's and see if anybody's around?"

Tess shrugged. "Sure, may as well," she said.

"Good flick, huh?"

"It was okay. The soundtrack was neat, and the part about the pool party was really funny." Her voice faded. In truth, the movie had depressed her, even though it was a comedy.

The film took place in Southern California, where everyone seemed to be tan and thin and beautiful. The teenagers all had shiny new cars and designer clothes and gold jewelry and no responsibilities except to have endless fun. Tess sighed. Dave had enjoyed the film. She didn't mean to take everything so personally.

"Don't sound so enthusiastic," Dave kidded her, squeezing her tightly against him as they approached his car. "You'd rather have seen that mystery, wouldn't you?"

"No, I wanted to see *Beachside High*. And I didn't *not* like it. I guess I just wish I could live the way those kids in the movie did."

"Don't we all? I sure wouldn't mind having a brand-new convertible. But L.A.'s one place, and Midvale's another, I guess," he said lightly, unlocking his old sedan.

"Stacy's house is as big as those houses," Tess reminded him. "And your folks don't exactly live in an old shack."

"It's not a mansion, either. That kid in the movie lived in a palace, Tess. A separate room just for the pool table, a living room with a grand piano, a four-car garage! Even the Harcourts can't match that."

"I'll bet in California, the servants have apartments bigger than our entire place out at the Estates," Tess remarked with a sigh.

Dave just laughed. "You really exaggerate sometimes, you know it? Your new place isn't that tiny. Besides," he added, "there's just the two of you."

"Thanks for reminding me," Tess told him tightly.

Dave took his hand off the wheel and turned toward Tess as he stopped for a red light. "Sorry, hon, I didn't mean it the way it came out," he assured her, cupping her chin in his hand and meeting her eyes with his clear gray ones. "I just hate to see you letting everything get you down." The light turned green, and Dave turned his attention to the road.

"Anyhow, if you want to see that other movie, we could catch it tomorrow afternoon."

"No, tomorrow's no good," Tess said quickly. "Um, Mom's made other plans for us. And I've got to get going on my French workbook."

"What're your mom and you doing?"

"Oh, nothing much," she answered airily. "Somebody she knows from work invited us over for an early dinner."

"Yeah?" Dave asked, waiting for the details.

But Tess didn't want anyone—not even Dave—to know her mother was dating Paul Holland's father, so she just said, "Yeah, and when I get home, I should head straight for my French book. If I've got to meet Alain Blanc on Monday, I don't want to seem like a totally hopeless case."

"How's cheerleading practice going? Easier cheers this season?"

"Yes, thank goodness! Stacy and Gina have been great. You know, I think they purposely kept the baseball cheers simple so I wouldn't have such a hard time. And so Kathy wouldn't. Sometimes I think the two of us are the only ones on that squad who couldn't make the Olympic gymnastics team. I'd give anything to be able to jump as high as Gina and Sherri. They can do arches that are practically backbends!"

"That's how Rich Stinson is this season," Dave said, pulling off the highway into the crowded parking lot of Nicola's. "I swear Rich could be blindfolded and still hit a ball straight between second and third base. He's bound to make the All-County Team this year. That means he'll be all-county in football, basketball, *and* baseball."

"Well, you're all-county in football and basketball *and* on the honor roll, so that makes you even, if not better off. Right? Kathy says that Rich can't seem to do better than straight C's in chemistry. And last year when he was still going with Stacy, she told me he had a hard time even getting C's in physics."

"He doesn't have to worry, though," Dave said good-naturedly. "He's already got his pick of scholarships."

"My dad told me that a friend of his in college broke his leg and got his football scholarship taken away while he was still in traction," Tess said. "I wouldn't want to have that hanging over my head, would you?"

"No way!" Dave agreed. "I just hope my right shoulder loosens up before next week's game with Carson. I don't want to hit grounders all day—or be pulled out of the lineup."

"Look, there's a space." Tess pointed. "Back to the left, next to that green van."

Dave backed up smoothly into the open space. "Looks like there's a real mob here tonight," he remarked as they walked across the lot. "Hope somebody's got a booth we can share."

On weekend nights Nicola's was always filled to capacity with Midvale kids and students from the state college. The pizza parlor had been a Midvale hangout since before Tess was born. No minimum was charged to sit at one of Nicola's worn Formica tables in a Naugahyde booth, and no song on the jukebox was over six months old. Unlike some Midvale restaurant owners, Bill and Patsy, who had bought the pizza parlor from Nicola years before, welcomed high-school students. Not only were prices always low, but the couple often came from behind the counter to catch up on the latest Midvale High gossip.

"Look, there's Gina and Tony," Tess said, spotting them as soon as she entered the pizza parlor. "We can sit with them."

Gina's face lit up when she saw Tess and Dave. "Good! We were hoping we'd see you two," she said, sliding over so Tony could move to her side of the booth.

"We went to the movies out at the mall," Tess explained. "What have you two been up to?"

"A party at the DiPietros' house, my parents' friends," Gina answered. "We ate beef rollatini, played a couple of games of Trivial Pursuit with the DiPietros' two little girls, then ducked out."

"Sounds like fun."

"How was the movie?" Tony asked.

"It was all right," Tess said. "Dave liked it

better than I did. To me, it just didn't seem real. All the kids were rich and gorgeous and went to parties all day long. I just couldn't relate to it."

A muffled chortle from the next booth caused Tess to turn. Valerie Masters, Midvale's head majorette, was rolling her icy blue eyes at Tif Rafferty and Joanie Gregson. "Can't relate to being rich and pretty, Tess?" Val drawled.

"No," Tess replied as sweetly as possible, though she could feel a flush of anger rising to her cheeks. "But maybe *you* should move to California right away. From what we saw on the screen tonight, you'd fit right in."

"Oh, I couldn't do that," Val replied without a pause. "I'm too crazy about our midwestern men to leave."

"Someday I'm going to bash her one," Tess muttered to Gina. Valerie smiled and winked at Dave, then turned back to her friends, the long honey-colored braid at the nape of her neck nearly swiping Tess's face.

"Don't let her get to you, Tess," Gina leaned across the table to whisper. "You know she'd give anything to trade places with you."

"Keep telling me, and maybe someday I'll believe it," Tess said dryly. At one time, Valerie's constant taunts had hurt her. Now she could usually ignore them, but Tess wished Val would relent once in a while. Valerie's malicious teasing was even more annoying when she had so many other problems.

"Um, are Stacy and Jeremy stopping by?" Dave's cheeks were pink from Val's attention. He nervously played with a stray lock of sandy hair that had fallen onto his forehead.

Gina shook her head. "I talked to Stacy on the phone this afternoon, and she said her sister had decided to come home from college for the weekend. So she and Jeremy were going to stay in and hang out with Sarah, I think."

"Coming to our baseball game next weekend, Tony?" As Dave spoke, he seemed to realize for the first time that he was fiddling with his hair. Quickly, he pushed it away from his face.

Tony, who attended a different school, shook his head. "I can't. Our first game's the same day. I'm the starting shortstop in the new lineup."

The guys started talking about sports then. Gina enthusiastically joined them. Tess made no effort to participate. As much as she loved Dave, she didn't feel like hearing him talk about baseball all night. She was beginning to wish they hadn't come to Nicola's. She'd much rather have been parked out by Brinton's Lake, feeling Dave's strong arms around her, his lips against hers, listening as he stroked her hair and told her how lucky he was to have her.

Her thoughts returned to Nicola's, and she was about to ask Gina the order of the cheers for next Saturday's game when a voice bellowed her name. Seeing who it was, she wished more than ever that she and Dave were somewhere besides Nicola's. Pushing away the slice of pizza the waitress had just brought her, she bent over her root beer, focusing all her attention on the straw. Maybe, just maybe, Paul Holland would take the hint and leave her alone.

She should have known better. "Tess Belding!" Paul shrieked. "I've been dying to see you!"

"You have been?" she asked evenly, keeping her voice and her eyes low, hoping he'd leave.

As usual, Paul appeared oblivious of the fact that he wasn't welcome. He stood at the end of the table, hanging onto the Formica with hands whose fingernails were chewed to the quick. Tess realized with a pang of alarm that Valerie Masters had swiveled toward the cheerleaders' table with obvious interest.

"I just wanted to tell you how excited my dad is that you and your mom are coming to dinner," Paul said loudly enough for everyone nearby to hear. "You're in for a real feast!" His close-set brown eyes seemed to gleam with the reflection of the pizzeria's stark fluorescent lights.

Somehow a tiny little voice managed to push its way through Tess's throat, but an unenthusiastic, "Great," was the only response she could produce.

"Yeah, you wouldn't believe a guy like my dad, who looks like a linebacker, could do all that delicate chopping and stuff," Paul went on, oblivious of Tess's discomfort. "He's so good with a meat cleaver, I told him I should call him 'the Beaver.' Get it? Beaver—like in Beaver Cleaver. *Leave It to Beaver*, you know?" He guffawed loudly. "Well, I'd better get back to the guys," he said at long last, gesturing toward a table full of sophomores. "Just wanted to let you know you were in for a treat. If you end up being my stepsister, you'll get to eat Chinese food any time you want!"

"Why didn't you just tell me you were having dinner at the Hollands' tomorrow?" Dave asked when Paul was out of earshot. "What's the big secret?" He shook his head, looking truly mystified.

"I just didn't think it made much difference where Mom and I were eating dinner," Tess said. She meant to sound nonchalant, but the harsh edge had crept into her voice once again.

"Does that mean your mother's dating?" Gina asked cheerfully. "That's terrific!"

"Yes, isn't it?" Tess said brightly. She turned to Dave, her voice unsteady. "Listen, I'm a lot more tired than I thought I was. Would you mind driving me home? You can come back if you want."

Dave made a face, as if he were about to protest, but when he turned to look at Tess, his manner changed abruptly. "Sure, we can go. But if you aren't going to eat that slice of pizza, I'll wrap it in a napkin and take it along."

"Sorry to be such a party pooper, guys." Tess managed to smile at Gina and Tony as she slid out of the booth. "It's been a long week."

"You look beat," Tony said kindly.

"Call me tomorrow," Gina requested.

"Oh, I will," Tess promised. "I'm sure I'll feel better in the morning."

Filled with relief, Tess turned toward the door. But as she and Dave passed the next booth, Valerie's low-pitched drawl assaulted her ears. "Really, Tif, can you imagine anything more perfect than Tess and Paul 'the pill' as sister and brother? Talk about a match made in heaven!"

Eyes glistening with tears, Tess walked on. But she had to wait for Dave at the door. He was stopping to say goodbye at half the booths.

"What's with you tonight?" Dave asked when he caught up with Tess. "You treat a harmless guy like Paul Holland as if he had the plague, you act as if Valerie's usual sarcastic remarks really bother you all of a sudden, and now you're glaring at me because I spoke to my friends. I know these haven't been the greatest few weeks in your life, Tess, but you've got to loosen up. You'll never shake off this depression if you don't even let yourself have   "

"Loosen up?" Her voice squ   stomped toward the car. "You mea   one big blast like those kids in the   in for a big surprise if you thin   and games, Dave Prentice!"

"Hey! Hold on!" He grabbed her arm. "I'm not trying to fight with you, you know. I just hate to see you let every little thing upset you this way."

"I'm not upset," she insisted, slowly enunciating each word. "Come on, let's get out of here."

"Okay." Shrugging, he pulled the car keys out of his pocket.

Sometimes even Dave is hopeless, Tess decided as she slid into the front seat, slamming the door behind her. He thought *she* was unreasonable for becoming angry at Val's endless taunts. He thought Paul Holland was a nice, harmless guy, and Tess was terrible for ignoring him.

Tess huddled in the corner as Dave turned the key and the engine kicked in. How could Dave care about her as much as he said he did and not understand her point of view? If he really loved her, he'd realize that Valerie Masters wouldn't be happy until she'd made Tess the laughingstock of Midvale High. He'd see that "harmless" Paul Holland was shooting off his mouth just so he could ride a cheerleader's coattails to popularity.

Tess was silent as Dave eased the car into the traffic on the highway. There was obviously no point in trying to explain herself. She might as well have been driving off with a stranger.

SEVEN

"What do you say, Tess? Think I could compete with the chef at the Golden Dragon?" Burt Holland asked as Tess pushed away her empty plate.

His deep voice pulled her back to reality and wiped away her contentment. Mr. Holland was far more talented with a wok than the Golden Dragon's chef, but she wasn't going to be won over so easily. "That was very good, thanks," she said. "How did you learn to cook Chinese food?"

"Glad you liked it," Mr. Holland said, smiling widely. Again, Tess wasn't taken in. The smile was intended for her mother, whom Burt Holland had gazed at intently since the Beldings had arrived.

"You should have tasted some of the junk Dad used to make," Paul said heartily. "Yuck! Crunchy pot roast in the middle of h potatoes and mushy broccoli."

Mr. Holland laughed. When he

again, Tess could tell his words, like his smile a moment before, were really for her mother. "Like too many men, it had never occurred to me that cooking was something to be shared and enjoyed by both sexes. I was your typical high-school boy, waited on hand and foot by my mother. In college, of course, I ate at the dorm. When I got married right after graduation, I didn't realize how lucky I was to have a wife who could cook. Laura's favorite room was the kitchen. That's one reason we both fell in love with this house, because it was half kitchen on the first floor."

"It's a super house," Tess agreed honestly. The Hollands lived on five acres of land next to Clover Farms Estates, in what had once been the main farmhouse for the land where the townhouse complex now stood. Fieldstone on the outside, the house was rustic yet comfortable on the inside. And the kitchen in which they sat was truly enormous, even bigger than the Harcourts'. But, unlike the kitchen at Stacy's, which was sparkling white and chrome, this one had an open hearth, high-beamed ceiling, and rough red-tile floor. Tess could imagine how much her mother, who'd loved to cook before she started working full time, would enjoy preparing a meal here.

"We redid this kitchen from top to bottom," Mr. Holland went on proudly. "It took us a long time, but we got just what we wanted." He gestured toward the detached island with its double oven, grill, range top, and microwave, above which scores of pots and pans and utensils dangled from circular wrought-iron hoops. "Being in real estate had plenty of advantages for me in that department, since I already knew the people who could do the best job of renovation."

He laughed again, but this time Tess thought he sounded a bit sad. "As much as I loved this kitchen, I never once thought of using it to cook for myself. That was Laura's domain, and she was tops. When she went into the hospital, I was lost in here. I couldn't even fry an egg without scorching it. When she never came home again—" He broke off, shaking his head, and when he spoke again, his voice was low.

"I was devastated, losing my wife so suddenly. At first, it was all I could do to heat up TV dinners for me and Paul. Then one day I snapped out of it and realized I had to do something. It wasn't fair to my son. He was just six then, and I knew I didn't want him growing up thinking that the family meal of the day was supposed to be something on a foil tray or out of a can. So I taught myself to cook."

"And succeeded admirably." Beth Belding's voice was soft.

"Not at first, though!" Mr. Holland was smiling again. "Paul's right about those first meals: they were grade A disasters! But I didn't give up. For one thing, I discovered that I genuinely liked to cook. And I liked good food too much to be satisfied with anything as mediocre as what I was whipping up."

He turned to Tess. "So, to get back to your original question, I started buying all the cooking magazines and studying them, the way you'd study a subject for school. Then, one summer, I decided Holland Realty could get by without me. I let my four salespeople handle all the work while I took lessons at a cooking school in Chicago."

"He doesn't just do Chinese, either," Paul put in. "He makes great chicken teriyaki and tacos and burritos and these French stews with wine in them and Indian curries so hot your mouth burns for days!"

"Well, I can still grill a mean burger and fry potatoes," Mr. Holland added with feigned humility. "I'm just a down-home boy from the plains at heart."

As she joined in the others' laughter, Tess found herself thinking that Burt Holland was really a pretty nice guy. He wasn't a bit like her own father, who was quiet and mostly serious. But Burt was genial and easygoing; he didn't talk down to her as if she were a kid. Still, she shuddered when she thought of Paul's remark at Nicola's. She didn't need this man for a stepfather—certainly not when drippy Paul Holland was part of the package.

Paul continued to dominate the conversation in his loud, aggressive voice. Tess studied him surreptitiously as he described to her mother, in step-by-step detail, the kitchen garden he and his father would soon begin planting behind the house. There wasn't a great deal of resemblance between Burt and Paul Holland. The father was as solid as an oak, while the son had a pudginess that made him look soft and unformed. Burt Holland's eyes were wide apart and warm, edged by crinkles of laughter. Paul's eyes were tiny, and he blinked constantly because of his contact lenses. When he'd arrived at Midvale High, he'd been a short, pimply boy with thick-lensed, horn-rimmed glasses. At least his looks had improved recently. But he'd been loud and brash ever since elementary school, the kind of kid who was instantly labeled the class clown by his fans and his foes.

Paul was once again trying to return the spotlight to himself, assuring Tess's mother, "Of course, I'm the one who convinced Dad we should grow our own veggies. I told him we could grow better stuff than what they rob you for in the supermarkets."

Her mother, like Mr. Holland, was listening attentively, nodding politely as if Paul weren't bragging outrageously.

As Tess continued her silent observation of the scene, she realized that she and her mother looked much less like each other than they once had. It was impossible to separate photos of Tess at age five from ones of her mother at the same age, except by the age of the photograph. They'd had the same long, straight brown hair and soft features. Tess's hair was no longer straight—in fact, she'd been perming it for so long, most people had forgotten her hair wasn't naturally curly. And Tess's hair had grown darker when she'd reached her teens, while her mother's had begun to gray.

There had been no gray in Beth Belding's hair since Tess had talked her into a henna treatment that had turned the gray into russet and gold highlights. But it would always be as straight as uncooked spaghetti, just as Mrs. Belding's makeup would always be more subdued than her daughter's. As she watched her mother, however, Tess saw a glow in her cheeks more luminous than any blusher could have provided. With a sinking heart, she wondered if her mother was falling in love with Burt Holland. Surely only love could have blinded her to how obnoxious the man's son was.

"Your mother tells me you're planning to be a bilingual secretary," Mr. Holland was saying to her.

"I hope so," Tess answered. "I'm going to have to bring my French grade up if I want to get into Winston. That's one of the few secretarial schools around here that offers bilingual courses," she explained. Looking at her watch in what she hoped was a casual, unstudied manner, she told him, "I've got a lot of studying to do in the next couple of weeks if I'm going to survive the midterm."

Mr. Holland nodded and pushed his chair

out a little way from the table. "It must be hard to have so much to do," he said sympathetically. "Being a cheerleader must be practically a full-time job in itself. And Paul tells me you're one of the best on the squad."

"Hardly." Tess set him straight with a laugh. Paul had obviously decided to impress her by praising her to his father. *Fat chance of that*, she thought. Aloud, she said, "I try to make up in enthusiasm what I lack in expertise."

"Atta girl! It's the spirit that counts. And if you've inherited your mother's, you've got plenty of it."

"I didn't know you'd known Mom very long," Tess said a little impatiently. She didn't need a virtual stranger to tell her what her own mother was like.

Her tone was lost on Mr. Holland. "Not as long as I wish I had," he said warmly. "But over the past month or so, Beth and I have gotten to know each other pretty well. There's a lot you can talk about over lunch."

"I guess there is," Tess said evenly. Her mother hadn't mentioned any lunches. She sat back in her chair, determined not to say another word until it was time to go. Clearly her contributions weren't needed to keep the conversation alive.

"Thanks again," she told Mr. Holland when she and her mother had put on their coats and stood at the door to say goodbye.

"See you in school, Tess," Paul brayed. "And don't tell too many of the other kids about my father the chef, huh? I don't want everyone in the whole school bugging me for an invitation!"

Tess smiled. Probably nothing would make Paul happier than for Tess to announce to the entire high school that she had eaten dinner at the Holland house.

"It was a pleasure meeting you, Paul," Mrs. Belding told him warmly. "I'm glad we got the chance to talk together. Burt, I'll dream about that meal!"

"Dream about me instead," he said in a low, intimate voice Tess didn't like. "I'll see you tomorrow at the shop."

Tess was silent as she got into the passenger side of her mother's compact wagon and they drove away. It was just six-thirty, and darkness was barely falling. She rolled down her window to savor the spring air.

"Burt's quite a cook, isn't he?" Hesitantly, her mother broke the silence.

"It was a good dinner," Tess agreed reluctantly. "But I don't see why you never told me you'd been having lunch with him all this time. Or don't I have a right to know what my own mother's doing?"

To Tess's surprise, her mother laughed cheerfully. "Sounds like you're the mother and I'm the daughter," she quipped. "I didn't mention Burt when I first met him simply because it

60

didn't seem important. He was just another customer. Even when he started taking me to lunch, he was still just a customer. We talked mostly about books and his house. He's a big do-it-yourselfer, and he was always stopping at the shop to browse through the books on home repair and renovation. I think he's done a lot of work on that house himself. Then, after Paul convinced him to put in a vegetable garden, he stocked up on gardening books. It wasn't until he asked me to dinner the other night that it hit me we weren't just salesclerk and client anymore."

Sure, Tess said to herself. Her mother made it sound as if everyone who wandered into The Bookworks took her out to lunch.

When Tess didn't respond, her mother asked, "What's wrong, dear? Don't you like Burt?"

Tess shrugged. "Sure, he seems nice enough. I guess I just didn't expect you to start—well, *dating* right away."

"Neither did I," her mother admitted. "But it *has* been about five months since your dad and I decided to divorce, Tess. And they've been a lonely five months," she added slowly. "I like Burt a lot. He's a good person, and he's fun, too. And he pretty much understands what I've gone through. It hasn't been easy for him raising Paul on his own."

"Raising Paul couldn't be easy under any circumstances," Tess said.

She felt the disapproval in her mother's quick sidelong glance. "I thought he seemed like a nice boy. Not the most with-it guy around perhaps, but he tries hard."

"Yeah, too hard," Tess retorted dryly.

"You've got to remember not everyone has your gift for making friends, Tess. Being popular doesn't come easy for everyone, and Paul's obviously had a pretty rough life."

For the rest of the drive home, Tess was silent. *What's happening to the people I love*, she wondered. First Dave and then her own mother had begun criticizing her—and sticking up for people like vicious Val and toady little Paul instead of coming to Tess's defense.

Her mother spoke as if being popular came naturally to Tess. She didn't seem to understand how hard Tess had worked—still worked—at being accepted by the kids when she was the only one in her crowd who was a techie. Tess worked twice as hard as the other girls on the squad to learn the cheer routines; she was *lucky* to be a cheerleader. And, in spite of the offhand way Tess complained about her French grades, there was a real chance she would fail her midterm and get kicked off the squad and—worse still—not get into the Winston School.

Mrs. Belding pulled the car into one of the assigned spaces at Clover Farms Estates, and the two of them walked wordlessly to their front door. Her mother obviously wasn't thinking about much except Burt Holland these days.

When they got to the townhouse, Tess went straight up to her room to work on some French translations, but her mind was elsewhere. As she read about the Côte d'Azur, the beautiful Riviera of Southern France, Tess once again lost herself in a fantasy. She saw herself stretched out on a yacht in the harbor at Saint-Tropez, basking in the sun and the admiring glances of the French boys who strolled or pedaled their bikes along the jetty.

She tried to concentrate on her work, but it was hopeless. The lure of her fantasy was too great. In her daydreams, Tess was carefree. They were a stark contrast to real life in Midvale, where the people closest to her no longer seemed to think about anyone but themselves.

EIGHT

Tess dressed for school Monday morning as if she were preparing to walk the plank. Mr. Calhoun was expecting her at his homeroom thirty minutes before the first bell so that he could introduce her to Alain Blanc.

Tess dreaded the meeting as much as a trip to the dentist. Ordinarily she'd have looked forward to meeting a French exchange student; it might have been a chance to find out more about the country where she hoped to work one day. But not now. She just didn't have the time— or the energy—to fit tutoring into her overloaded schedule or her overburdened brain. And the way things had been going, Alain was sure to be a nerd. Her good luck seemed to have deserted her.

For a brief moment Sunday evening as she dressed for bed, she had entertained the hope that Alain might have refused Mr. Calhoun's request to tutor her. But she'd quickly abandoned that notion. After all, he was the Calhouns' house guest, so he wouldn't feel he had much choice.

Resigned to her fate, Tess took extra care as she dressed. Alain Blanc might be a nerd, but she didn't want him thinking she was the same type. She'd chosen her outfit after a careful consideration of almost everything in her closet. The charcoal twill pants were cut very tight from the knee to the ankle, a style she considered rather French and sleek. The pale gray, lace-up jazz shoes would make her look fashionable, and the royal blue camp shirt matched both her eyes and her eyeshadow. She topped it with Dave's letter sweater: the blue and gold pulled the other items together and the sweater would advertise to Alain Blanc that she had a boy-friend, just in case he was tempted to get the wrong idea.

She'd gulped down half a glass of milk and was grabbing a sweet roll to gobble in the car when her mother, still in her robe and slippers, came downstairs.

"You're up bright and early today," her mother said through a yawn, heading straight across the kitchen to flick the button on the coffeemaker. "And don't tell me you're going off to school with a Danish for breakfast! Why didn't you have a bowl of cereal or some eggs, for goodness' sake?"

"I don't have time today," Tess answered, taking a big bite of the pastry. "I've got to be at school early to meet this French guy who's supposed to tutor me. I have cereal every other day of the week, Mom. It's not going to kill me to eat a Danish in the car this one time."

"I guess not. And it doesn't look as if you'll be eating it in the car, either," Mrs. Belding observed as Tess washed down the last bite of her roll with a final swallow of milk.

"You should be relieved. Now I'll be driving with two hands," Tess said pertly as she scooped up the books she'd set on the counter. "I'd better get going. Anything special I should do for dinner?"

Her mother opened the freezer door and studied the contents, then closed it again, shaking her head. "Nothing in there really turns me on," she admitted. "Why don't we both take a break from cooking tonight? I'll stop on the way home from the shop and pick up some burgers and fries. You don't have practice this afternoon, do you?"

"Nope, tomorrow. I'll be here when you get home, Mom." The image of Mr. Calhoun and the faceless Frenchman loomed in her mind. "Have a good day at work," she said as she hurried out of the house.

After she parked in the student lot, Tess checked her makeup in the rear-view mirror. Then she grabbed her books, hurried to the front door of the building, and walked briskly to Mr. Calhoun's classroom before she could change her mind. She took a deep breath as she stood in front of the doorway, then reached for the knob and pushed the door open.

Mr. Calhoun was seated behind the desk, talking to a short, overweight kid wearing clothes that looked as if they'd been slept in. Tess gasped in dismay. *Oh, no,* she thought, *he's even worse than I feared!* Then the boy looked up at her, and she saw that he was a sophomore she had seen in the hallways. As she closed the door behind her, he muttered something to the teacher.

"Work out those examples tonight, then bring them in tomorrow morning at the same time," Mr. Calhoun said pleasantly while the boy frantically gathered up his papers and notebooks. He was so flustered that Tess momentarily forgot her own nervousness.

"Ah, Tess! Good to see you." Mr. Calhoun got to his feet with a welcoming smile.

"Morning, Mr. Calhoun," she said, finding it easy to smile now. *Maybe Alain Blanc changed his mind and isn't coming to Midvale after all,* she thought. Then she realized that the French teacher was looking away from her, toward the back of the room.

She shifted her gaze, and noticed for the first time another boy, sitting quietly, reading *Rolling Stone.* He, too, got to his feet, and it was all Tess could do not to gasp for the second time since entering the room.

67

Alain Blanc was gorgeous—definitely a positive addition to the male population at Midvale High, from his blond short-cropped hair to the high-topped white sneakers he wore with a pair of baggy paratrooper pants and a baggy green cotton sweater.

"Alain, *viens ici! Je te présente Mademoiselle* Tess Belding," Mr. Calhoun called as Alain walked over to meet them.

Don't tell me he expects us to speak in French all the time, Tess thought in a panic. *I have enough trouble thinking in French as it is—I'll never be able to do it while I'm looking at this gorgeous guy!*

She was grateful when Alain said in English, "It is a pleasure to meet you." But even her command of English failed her, and she could only smile in reply.

Mr. Calhoun saved her. "You two can work out just how you want to go about this thing." He gestured toward a group of seats. "Why don't we sit down for a few minutes and discuss it?"

"After you." Alain inclined his head in a gesture Tess found romantically chivalrous. His accent was authentically Parisian—"Af-tair yu." His soft tenor voice was throaty and sexy.

"Alain said he'd be glad to tutor you," Mr. Calhoun told Tess when they were seated. "Twice a week on a regular schedule might be a good way to start. Then you can figure out if you need more or less help."

Tess nodded, thinking it might not be so difficult to find time for two tutoring sessions a week. Alain told her, "When Monsieur Calhoun asked if I would be able to help you with your studies, I realized this would be an excellent method in which for me to practice my English."

"But your English seems perfect!" Tess said breathlessly. *So does the rest of you*, she added silently, gazing at his short, straight nose, squared-off jawline, and high forehead. A crescent-shaped scar cut through his right eyebrow and ran almost to his hairline. It was faint, but even so, it had the effect of balancing out the delicacy of his small mouth and ivory skin. The result was undeniably handsome.

"*Mais non!*" He chuckled, the laugh lines deepening around his eyes. "Monsieur Calhoun says you are having trouble with the idioms and irregular verbs of my language. I, too, have difficulty with the American slang. For example" —he rolled his eyes, which Tess found terribly Gallic and charming—"yesterday I said to somebody, 'Trap you later,' when I should have said, 'Catch you later.'"

Tess laughed with him, and began eagerly confessing her own idiomatic blunders. In the light of Alain's gentle sense of humor, her own slips of the tongue no longer seemed so embarrassing.

Mr. Calhoun broke in after checking his watch. "Perhaps you two should try to set up a time for your first meeting now."

"After school isn't great," Tess said thoughtfully. "I've got cheering practice twice a week, and I usually have to get dinner started at home. How about Sundays and one evening after dinner—maybe Wednesdays? I'll have to check with my mom. I can let you know tomorrow," she told Alain.

"Wednesday and Sunday would be good," he said.

"What classes are you taking?" Tess asked. "You're probably not in any of mine, but if you are, I can let you know then."

As it turned out, none of their classes were the same. Except for French and English, all Tess's classes were in the vo-tech wing. But they did share a third-period study hall.

"Oh, that's good!" Tess said happily after they'd compared schedules. Hearing the eagerness in her voice, she added, "I mean, it will be easy for us to make plans for tutoring then."

"Yes." Alain continued to stare at his schedule, a slight frown crinkling his forehead. "This is very confusing to me, I'm afraid. It is not at all the way we study at the *lycée* in Paris."

"Oh, you'll get used to it," she assured him. "Once you learn your way around the building, it's a breeze. And the five minutes between classes are more than enough time to switch books at your locker and get to where you're going."

"I want to learn all there is about America

and going to school here," Alain said enthusiastically. "Monsieur Calhoun tells me you will participate in the assembly you call a pep rally during the last period of school on Friday."

"You don't have pep rallies in France? It's sort of a cheering session to get everyone's spirits up for our first baseball game the next afternoon."

"Ah, I see." He nodded solemnly. "And you are a leader of the cheers, *non*?"

"A cheerleader, right. There are six of us on the varsity squad. We get out in front in our uniforms—the school colors—and lead cheers against the opposing team. This season is baseball. Do you play that in school in France?"

"No, but I am familiar with the baseball, and I like it. At home, I play football—what you here call soccer—and also lacrosse."

They were interrupted by the sound of Mr. Calhoun clearing his throat. "If you two have everything decided, I think I'll do some work on my teaching plan before the first bell."

"Oops, I'd better get to my own homeroom!" Tess jumped up. "Can I help you find your homeroom, Alain?"

"I am right here, so I do not have to move yet. Not until . . . let's see. My first-period physics class."

"That'll be downstairs in the science labs," Tess told him. "You just go out the door here and take the stairs at the end of the hall to the right."

"Very good." He grinned, showing small, even white teeth. "And I will be seeing you in our study hall, *non*?"

"You will be seeing me in our study hall, *oui*." Tess giggled, wondering how she ever could have been so nervous about meeting Alain. He was just what this gloomy spring needed. "See you then," she said merrily, bouncing to the door. She had to stop when Dave's sweater caught on the back of the chair. She disentangled herself quickly, glancing to see if Alain had seen her clumsy exit. But his blond head was already bent again over *Rolling Stone*. Alain looked a lot like a younger version of Sting. She turned and hurried out, getting to her locker just as the first bell for homeroom started to clang.

She hung the sweater on a hook inside and started shuffling books around, pulling out those she'd need for her morning classes. But her mind was still in Mr. Calhoun's homeroom with Alain. What a doll he'd turned out to be— and a genuine Parisian, too! *You can tell at a glance he's not a Midvale boy*, she thought. His clothes, his style, the way he carried himself were far too sophisticated to have sprung from central Illinois.

His accent sent a tingle up her spine. His English was so charming, too. The way he said "the baseball" instead of just "baseball" was adorable.

"I joost luv ze bazeball myself," she said under her breath as she closed the locker door. By the time she reached her own homeroom, she had a silly smile on her face that couldn't be wiped away.

NINE

Tess was heading toward her third-period study hall, eager to see Alain and find out how he'd liked Midvale High so far, when someone grabbed her elbow from behind.

"I've been dying to see you!" It was Stacy, her pretty face animated and flushed. "I got a look at our new exchange student—he sits across from me second period—and, wow, he's really something! You lucky thing!"

"Stacy, my relationship with Alain is going to be strictly business. I *am* going with Dave, remember?"

"Oh, sure," Stacy answered lightly. "But that doesn't mean a girl can't look, does it? I mean, I'm crazy about Jeremy, but I don't shut my eyes when I see a real hunk. Alain is at least a nine in my book. I'd say a ten if he hadn't ignored me completely."

Tess laughed. "I guess he is pretty good-looking, isn't he?"

"Mm-hmm," Stacy agreed. "He's not handsome in an average American way, though. He's just got something that makes him stand out in a crowd," she explained, echoing Tess's own opinion.

"Like Erik?" Tess teased.

"Oh, you!" Stacy gave her a playful punch in the arm. "Anyway, I just wanted to let you know I'd set eyes on the new arrival and was impressed. Plenty of foreign intrigue there."

"As long as he's a good tutor—that's what's important to me."

"I'll bet he could teach you all sorts of things," Stacy cooed provocatively before she broke up in a fit of giggles. "Look, I'll see you in the cafeteria at lunch, okay?" She raised an eyebrow. "*Au revoir*."

Alain walked into the large study hall a few minutes after Tess, just under the bell, so she was able to watch the reactions of the assembled class as he entered, smiling shyly. It was clear that most of the students had heard about the arrival of Alain Blanc. Many eyes watched him with blatant curiosity. Alain seemed unaware that he was the object of mass scrutiny. His gaze picked Tess out of the crowd, and he smiled warmly, raising one hand slightly in greeting. She'd thought of saving him a seat when she entered, but had been afraid that might look presumptuous. Now she wished she had. Alain's eyes darted about in her general vicinity, as if looking for a place. Seeing none, he flashed her another smile, then returned to the back of the room and found a seat there.

Tess concentrated as hard as she could on her French workbook during the period. When the bell rang, she was on her feet instantly, hurrying back to where Alain was still seated.

"How's it going?" she asked brightly. "Getting the hang of high school American-style?"

"So far, I like it." His eyes widened. "Everything is so—what is the word?—so casual here. Not at all like the *lycée* back home."

"Are the teachers awfully strict there?"

He shrugged. "I never thought so before, but compared to the teachers here, I'd say so. This is more like summer camp."

Tess grinned. "I never think of it that way. I suppose I'd be in real trouble if I lived in France. I'm having enough trouble here."

"I think you are not fair to yourself," Alain said timidly, rising and grabbing his books. "From what Mr. Calhoun told me, you are considered the finest of all the girls in the secretarial course. He says only with the French lessons do you have a problem."

"That's a big one, believe me," Tess assured him ruefully. They had reached the corridor, and Alain fumbled with his binder to extricate his class schedule. "Where do you have to go next?" She leaned toward him to look at the schedule. "Phys ed? That's easy. You just go down to the first floor and look for the big double doors to the gym. Go inside and walk all the way to the back of the gymnasium and you'll see the sign for the boys' locker room. Do you have gym clothes?"

He nodded. "I'll have to stop at my locker to pick them up. I am eager to play the American sports. I wonder what we'll be doing."

"I can answer that question. It's spring, and that means you'll be playing the baseball." She smiled as she said it.

"*Ah, oui?* Yes, that should be very interesting!"

"Have fun," she called after him as he hurried off. Still smiling, she turned to head in the opposite direction—and bumped hard into Dave.

She jumped, but Dave just said genially, "That's your new tutor, isn't it? He's in my physics class. Seems like a nice guy."

"Doesn't he?" Tess agreed, feeling silly.

"See? All this time you were worrying for nothing, thinking he was going to turn out to be some slob. And what did you end up with? A regular guy."

"He speaks French beautifully, too. Such a perfect accent!" Tess enthused as they started walking down the hall. "I'm sure I can get it all together if he helps me."

"Now you're sounding more like optimistic Tess," Dave said approvingly, ruffling her hair. "Hey, do you think you could make it to Nicola's after school today? Seems like we never get to see much of each other these days."

"As a matter of fact, I can," Tess told him

happily. "Mom's bringing dinner home with her, so there's no reason for me to rush off. I *should* go straight home and study my French, but—"

"But?" Dave stopped and slung his arm around her, pulling her close.

"But I'd much rather be with you," she murmured. "Besides," she added as he kissed the top of her head, "with a real native like Alain coaching me, I don't expect to have much trouble with French in the future."

"That's my girl!" He released her. "I may not see you after your French class. If I don't, I'll just catch you at Nicola's, all right?"

She nodded, then watched him hurry down the stairs. *What a lucky girl I am*, she told herself as she slowly continued down the corridor. Dave was truly terrific. He was good-looking, smart, a terrific athlete, and one of the kindest, most sensitive human beings she'd ever met.

For the rest of the day Tess felt as if her luck had returned. Dave was his sweet, normal self again, and Alain had turned out to be anything but a nerd. If his teaching was as good as his looks, Tess would soon be passing French with high marks.

At lunch, she couldn't help basking in the envy of the other girls who had encountered Alain Blanc's Gallic charms. "Stacy's right. Foreign men *are* more exotic," Gina said with a chuckle. "Half the girls in Midvale have an eye on your new tutor."

"That's right," Stacy agreed. "If I were you,

Tess, I wouldn't turn my back on some of these girls after they find out Alain's going to be spending so much time with you."

"Two sessions a week," Tess protested, but no one seemed to hear her.

"I liked him the minute I saw him. His hair's almost as short as mine." Janet Perry's eyes gleamed impishly behind her aviator glasses.

"You're not the only one who liked him," Marsha Steiner put in. "And it wasn't just his haircut they were checking out, either. I was walking behind him down the corridor this morning when Valerie Masters came from the other direction, and you should have seen the look she gave him! Her eyes nearly popped out of her head."

"I'm sure Alain's too smart to fall for Valerie's act," Tess said when they'd stopped chuckling.

"Who isn't?" Stacy asked, flipping her long hair behind her shoulder. "It shouldn't take too long for any half-awake guy to figure her out. You know, that guy Cal—the one in college who took her to the Winter Carnival Ball—really liked her, but she treated him like dirt."

"I still can't believe Val and Dex haven't gotten together yet," Gina remarked. "I think that would be the perfect match."

"Do you?" Janet asked, shaking her head. "They'd be at each other's throats in about a week. They both want too much of the attention for themselves."

"They are best buddies, you know," Tess reminded them. "Only, I can't see them as anything but friends. They can be friends because they're so much alike, but it'll never go any deeper for the same reason."

"I agree," Stacy said.

"You don't really think she could get her claws into poor Alain, do you?" Tess asked. "He's much too nice for that, I think. But he's a foreigner. Maybe he's never met a girl like Valerie before."

Gina laughed. "Come on, Tess, the French invented the art of flirting."

"Anyhow—" The bell announcing the end of the period interrupted Janet. "Any guy more than twelve years old can get Valerie's number within ten minutes. And I don't just mean her phone number. Who's going to be heading over to Nicola's after school? Dennis and I have a project to finish up for the *Sentinel*, but we're going to stop by afterward if we've got the time." All talking at once, they took their trays and headed to the cafeteria's drop-off window.

Tess was worried again as she headed for her afternoon classes. If she had one enemy in the world, it was Valerie Masters. Tess had tried in the beginning to be friends, but Valerie clearly wouldn't be content until she'd made Tess miserable. Vicious Val would like nothing better than to sweep Tess's tutor off his feet and out of Tess's life.

But Valerie was already getting enough

laughs at Tess's expense. *Just let her try*, Tess told herself. *I met him first, and he's my tutor*. If Val Masters thought she was going to snatch up Alain Blanc, she was in for a big surprise!

TEN

Dave wasn't at Nicola's when Tess got there. Of the regular crowd, only Patricia Petersen, who was sitting by herself at a booth in the back, had arrived. She motioned for Tess to join her.

"Meeting Dave?" she asked.

Tess nodded. "Is Brent coming by?"

Patricia shook her carroty shag. "Nope, he's working after school now. Didn't I tell you? He's doing three afternoons a week at that ice-cream place across from the mall. I wish he'd find something else. Every time I stop in to see him, I have a double dip. I'll be as big as a house soon!"

"I wouldn't lose sleep worrying if I were you," Tess told her. Patricia, a junior, was the smallest cheerleader on the squad, barely past the five-foot mark. As far as Tess could tell, there wasn't an excess pound on her wiry little body. "This place sure is dead today, isn't it?" Tess looked around. "I'm not used to coming here in the afternoons anymore. What's happened to everybody?"

"We're early," Patricia assured her. "Just wait, in ten or fifteen minutes, the place will be hopping."

"What's happening with your folks?" Tess asked. When her parents first separated, Tess spent a lot of time confiding in Patricia, the only other girl on the squad whose parents had divorced. Patricia had taken the breakup hard, especially when her mother started going to singles bars, and her father started dating women who, frequently, weren't much older than his daughter.

"They're back to normal, thank goodness!" Patricia heaved a sigh of relief. "Mom says she sees now how shallow the singles scene is. She goes out with this divorced lawyer once in a while, but it's nothing serious. And Dad's decided women a lot younger than he is are too immature. Would you believe it, he's seeing a woman who's even got some gray hairs?" Patricia laughed. "What's up with your parents?"

Tess shrugged. "My dad's moving to California next week. He's taking me to brunch on Sunday." She laughed shakily. "Like a casual acquaintance, you know? That's how he's been treating me. I've talked to him on the phone but he hasn't come to the house once since moving day. As for Mom—I'm not sure." Tess shook her head. "She seems happy enough, but I don't get to see much of her now that she's working full time. She's dating, um, some guy, too."

"Isn't she going out with Paul Holland's father?"

"Oh, no!" Tess groaned. "Don't tell me it's all over school already!"

"What's the big deal?" Patricia seemed puzzled. "I've met Mr. Holland a couple of times—he helped Dad when he was trying to find a new place to live—and he seemed pretty neat to me. What's wrong with him?"

"Nothing, as far as I can tell," Tess admitted, "except for the fact that he happens to be Paul's father. I mean, how would you like it if that jerk was going around telling everyone who'd listen that you and he might be related someday?"

Patricia laughed. "Paul's too much, isn't he? He just doesn't know when to stop sometimes. But he's not that bad, Tess."

"Easy for you to say," Tess muttered. She was happy to see Sherri coming through the door from the street with Jill Heilman, one of the junior majorettes. Dave was close on their heels. "I'd better get a booth for Dave and me," she said, slipping toward the aisle. "Then Sherri and Jill can sit with you."

Patricia nodded pleasantly as Tess took an empty booth across the aisle. Tess leaned over the Formica tabletop and motioned to show Dave where she was.

"Hey, Tess." Dave slid his broad-shouldered body into the booth across from her. "Sorry I'm late, but I ran into one of your admirers by the lockers and couldn't get away."

"Who's that?" Tess asked eagerly, wondering if Dave had spoken to Alain Blanc about her.

"Paul Holland. Who else?" he asked, his eyes twinkling.

"Pardon my enormous ego, but I was under the impression that Paul wasn't the only boy in the whole school who admired me," she said sarcastically.

"Uh-oh! Guess I said the wrong thing," Dave said easily. "You shouldn't be so sensitive about the kid, Tess. Paul thinks you're the greatest thing in the world."

"I'll bet he does. What was he talking to you about—or was he just issuing an advance invitation to our parents' wedding?"

Dave laughed, even though Tess wasn't cracking a smile. "All he wanted was to say he hoped I didn't mind that he and his father monopolized your time the other day."

"What did he think you were going to do?" Tess snorted with indignation. "Challenge him to a duel?"

"The kid just wants people to like him," Dave argued.

"He should!" Tess retorted. "And would you stop calling him 'the kid' all the time? He's practically the same age as us!"

"Oooookay," Dave said slowly, trying to sound like Johnny Carson. "I guess that's one subject we don't discuss. Forget I mentioned him."

"It's perfectly all right to mention him," Tess said stubbornly.

Now it was Dave's turn for sarcasm. "As long as I put him down, right? Sorry, Tess, I'm not going to say things I don't mean just to make you happy."

A deadening silence descended over their booth, broken only when the waitress came to take their order. *How did things get off to such a bad start?* Tess wondered. She couldn't understand the change in Dave. He knew she'd been upset lately, yet he seemed to be looking for opportunities to scold her. He frequently complained that they didn't have enough time together anymore, then he acted as if he'd rather be with almost anybody else.

She was grateful when Stacy and Jeremy entered. "Here, come sit with us!" she called.

"Hey, Jer, Stace," Dave said gruffly as he dragged himself out of the booth and to his feet and swung around to sit next to Tess.

Tess did her best to act calm and casual, spiritedly discussing Midvale's chances at the upcoming baseball game. But she was careful to direct her comments to Stacy and Jeremy and not to Dave. Dave was talking cheerfully to Tess as well as the others, just as if he hadn't been snarling at her a few minutes earlier. But she couldn't forget his insensitivity so easily.

If this is what Dave's going to be like, I don't

mind being stuck at home so much of the time, she told herself. Of course, she knew she didn't really mean it. Even when she was angry with him, she liked being close to him like this, feeling the warmth of his body through his long-sleeved striped jersey as he sat with one arm flung across the back of the seat behind her.

"Our practice tomorrow isn't going to interfere with your tutoring, is it, Tess?" Stacy asked suddenly, her voice gentle with concern.

"Alain and I aren't having our first tutoring session till Wednesday, and that's after dinner," Tess answered. "The only thing that might interfere with my concentration at practice is thinking about what feast I'm going to cook up for dinner afterward." She sighed, then smiled. "At least Mom's picking up burgers on the way home from work today! Otherwise, I wouldn't be here."

"Poor Tess!" Stacy said with feeling. "I wouldn't want to be in your shoes. Emma hasn't given up on me yet, but I'd be helpless by myself. I can't imagine what I'd do if I had to race home from school every day to cook an entire meal from scratch. Make TV dinners, I suppose."

"TV dinners would end up costing a lot of money, even for just the two of us," Tess told her. She didn't bother to tell Stacy that fixing dinner usually involved preheating the oven, popping in something her mother had prepared ahead of time, and making a salad. She still had to be home to babysit the meal, and that task put a big crimp in most of her plans. With a full-time housekeeper on the premises, Stacy didn't even have to make her bed if she didn't feel like it. All she had to do was have fun—like those kids in *Beachside High*.

As if conjured up by Tess's memory of the movie, Valerie Masters swept into Nicola's with Dex Grantham at her heels. Joanie Gregson and Tif Rafferty had come in earlier with Howie Fellows, a buddy of Dex's and a sometime date of Tif's. Valerie and Dex headed toward their friends—then Valerie made a detour just to pass Tess's booth.

"Hi, guys," she drawled. "All set for Friday's pep rally?"

Tess ignored her, wishing Dave would also refuse to acknowledge Valerie. Instead, he was the first to speak. "You bet!" he said. "The team's raring to go. If Stinson doesn't strike out every batter at the plate, I'll be surprised. His arm's better than ever this year."

"We've got two more practices before the rally," Stacy explained. "But the squad looks pretty good."

"Oh?"

Valerie's voice rose gently to convey a tinge of doubt. Tess felt the other girl's ice-blue eyes dart in her direction. Even when she didn't say something cutting, Val made her opinion clear.

"We've got a great new cheer just for baseball season," Tess said, looking Valerie straight in the eye and smiling with confidence. "I love it."

"That's nice." Valerie smiled thinly, then turned back to Stacy. "Wait until you see the new twirling routine I've worked out for the majorettes. It's super! Ms. Bowen came to watch us at practice today, and she took me aside to tell me I was the best head majorette she'd seen at Midvale."

"She hasn't been teaching here long, has she?" Tess asked sweetly.

Valerie wasn't about to let a put-down slip by. "I'm sure she still knows who's good," she said, her voice so cool Tess could almost see the icicles dripping off the words. "And who's *not*, of course."

Tess knew she should let Valerie have the last word, but she was too angry to stop. "What a shame the majorettes are so good this season when they don't get to perform at the games," she said, again looking Valerie straight in the eye. "It must really bum you out that you've worked so hard for nothing. After all, the pep rally's not quite the same as the game, is it?"

"I'd hardly say it's a waste of time," Valerie said acidly. "A cheerleader should realize how important it is to keep the school spirit high at a rally, Tess."

"Oh, I do!" Tess insisted. "And I really think it's a shame the band doesn't perform during baseball season." She giggled as Val glared. "Then again, I suppose you'd look awfully silly high-stepping around a baseball diamond."

When Val didn't answer, an awkward silence fell on the table.

"How come no one ever gets excited about the swim or tennis teams?" Dex finally demanded, determined as usual to command his fair share of attention. He cleared his throat ostentatiously. "In case everyone's forgotten, I do happen to be the star of both of them."

"Maybe that's why no one ever gets excited," Valerie drawled, and even Tess laughed. Valerie could be pretty funny with her sarcasm, it was true; but when she taunted Tess, the note of good humor disappeared from her voice. True to form, when the laughter ended, she turned back to Tess and asked archly, "Oh, by the way, Tess, where's Paul Holland today?"

"How should I know? Do I look like his nursemaid?"

"Oh, sorry." Valerie's eyes widened in a caricature of surprise. "I didn't mean to say the wrong thing. I just thought the two of you were like this." She held up her right hand with the fingers crossed.

"You must have me mixed up with somebody else," Tess said lightly, grinning over Valerie's head at Dex, who was winking at her and flashing his perfectly straight white teeth in a smile that mocked Valerie's waspishness.

"Well, the gang's waiting for us, so we'd better join them. Come along, Dexter," Valerie said, grasping Dex's arm and leading him regally across the floor.

Tess sat back with a satisfied smile. She knew she'd managed to get under Val's skin this time—Valerie called Dex "Dexter" only when she was irritated.

"That Valerie's something else, isn't she?" Dave asked in what sounded to Tess like admiration. "She sure knows how to get Grantham, doesn't she?"

"She's a real laugh riot." Tess's voice was steely.

"I saw you laugh when she made that remark about Dex," Dave said accusingly. "Or is it only when you're the target that you don't think she's funny?"

"It's different when she picks on me," Tess argued.

Stacy sprang to her friend's defense. "Valerie really does go after Tess with her claws out, Dave."

Dave shrugged. "If you really think she's singling you out, wouldn't it help if you were nicer to her? That comment of yours about Ms. Bowen really started things today."

"I couldn't win with Val no matter what I did or said," Tess tried to explain. Then she gave up. Dave was astonishingly blind to some people's nasty ways. "I'd better head for home," she said, taking some singles from her wallet and putting them on the table for her part of the check.

Dave stood up to let her out of the booth. "I'll walk you to your car."

"Don't bother," Tess said. "I'm going to have to hustle to get some homework done before Mom gets home. I'll talk to you later." Dave shrugged and sat down again.

Tess said goodbye to everyone, waving to people as she passed on the way out.

At home she hurried upstairs and changed into the sweat suit and mocs she liked to wear around the house. Then she sat down on her bed, propped herself up on the pillows, and opened her French text. For once, she had no problem studying or concentrating on the words in front of her. The memory of Alain's accent made the language seem more real to her. And she couldn't afford to let her mind wander if she didn't want to humiliate herself in front of Alain on Wednesday.

She worked so diligently that by the time she heard her mother come in downstairs, she'd done all her homework for the evening.

"Chow time!" her mother called loudly, laughing when she realized Tess was already halfway down the stairs.

"Here I am," Tess told her. "And I could eat a horse."

"Well," Mrs. Belding answered, "these may not be the greatest burgers in the world, but I do think they're real beef."

"Delicious!" Tess said a few minutes later as they sat across from each other at the table in the dining area. "All the better for not having cooked them myself."

"Not bad, are they?" her mother agreed. "This is our splurge for the week, so enjoy every morsel. I think I'll get chicken-in-the-pot ready for tomorrow. How does that sound to you?"

"It's fine with me," Tess answered off-handedly, distracted by the TV listings she was perusing. "Hey, there's a good movie on tonight. At least it sounds good. A made-for-TV mystery, starting at eight."

"Don't you have homework to do?" Mrs. Belding asked.

"Nope. It's all done already." Tess couldn't help sounding pleased with herself.

"Good girl! It's been a while since the two of us just curled up and watched the tube together. I should be finished with the chicken by the time the movie starts." She got up and walked toward the kitchen. "Oh, by the way, how was your French tutor? Did you meet him today?"

"Uh-huh. Our first tutoring session's Wednesday. He's terrific," she said enthusiastically. "I have a feeling Alain Blanc is going to make a big difference."

ELEVEN

Mrs. Belding told Tess on Tuesday morning that she'd accepted Burt Holland's invitation to dinner and a movie on Wednesday. "Do you know, I didn't realize until he invited me that it's been over a year since I've set foot in a movie theater?" she asked in surprise.

Tess warned her to avoid *Beachside High*, then reminded her mother she'd scheduled a tutoring session for Wednesday evening. "Do you mind if Alain and I have our lesson here?" she asked. "I'd hate to have to go over to the Calhouns' house. I'd feel funny working on my French accent with the teacher right there."

"No, it's fine for the two of you to study here," her mother replied. "You know I've always trusted you, Tess."

"This is strictly business, anyhow," Tess assured her.

"Even if it weren't—even if it were Dave who was coming over—I'd trust you."

"Thanks, Mom," Tess said, adding lightly, "I trust you, too."

As Tess drove to school, she wondered if her lighthearted declaration had been true. She couldn't decide if she really trusted her mother with Burt Holland.

Tess had enjoyed the previous evening. "Just us girls," her mother had remarked when the two of them were propped up against the headboard of the king-sized bed in her mother's bedroom, cold drinks on the bedside tables and a big bowl of freshly popped corn between them.

Tess had become so involved in the movie that she completely forgot to call Dave. But he called at ten o'clock, just as the TV show ended, and was cheerful and attentive. He didn't mention Paul Holland or Valerie Masters. Instead, they talked about the party Stacy was throwing at her house after Saturday's game. When she hung up, Tess was both happy and puzzled. How could she have been angry with Dave? He was the most understanding guy on earth. Although she had been the one who forgot to call, Dave acted almost apologetic, as if it were his fault.

So Tess was happy to let her mother spend an evening with Burt Holland. Tess herself was planning to spend several hours with a sexy Frenchman.

The day got even better when Alain went out of his way to secure a seat next to hers in study hall. "I ran all the way down the hall so we would have time to talk before the bell rang," he told her loudly enough for the entire class to hear. "I wanted to remind you to do that translation in your workbook for tomorrow's lesson."

"It's all done already," she said confidently. "Do I get an automatic A?"

They talked until the final bell rang, pausing when several class members came over to them. Tess was flattered that Alain had hurried to talk to her, and she wasn't entirely sure he'd just wanted to check on that French exercise. Alain seemed genuinely attracted to her; he looked at her intently as he spoke. Some of the other girls in the room seemed to share her suspicion. Several had stared as she and Alain chatted, probably wishing they were in her seat.

Her good mood carried her through the rest of the day. At cheering practice, Stacy commented, "You sure are energetic today, Tess. Your jumps are looking superprofessional, too. I guess that cheering seminar you took at the end of basketball season is paying off."

"I learned a lot there. All those college cheerleaders! You wouldn't believe how talented some of them are, Stacy. They weren't just cheerleaders—they were gymnasts. I could never be that good."

"Maybe not. But at least cheering is important enough to you that you spent your savings for a seminar. Nobody else around here did."

Tess giggled. "That's because nobody else needed one quite so much. I still consider myself lucky to be on the squad in the first place. Tess Belding, Midvale's only cheerleader with two left feet!"

"You're too hard on yourself. You've only got one and a half left feet," Stacy teased.

When the squad members were changing out of their practice clothes in the locker room, Stacy again remarked on Tess's cheerful disposition. "Sure it's just good cheering that's filled you with good cheer?" she asked.

"As opposed to what?"

"I don't know. An exotic Frenchman sweeping you off your feet, for instance."

"Don't be silly, Stacy!" Tess laughed, but she could feel her cheeks starting to burn.

"How does Dave feel about Alain tutoring you?"

"He thinks anything that'll make me stop worrying about my grades all the time is a good thing, I suppose. Why?"

Stacy gave her a look of disbelief. "Most guys would be jealous if their girlfriends were going to be cozying up to another boy twice a week. And if the guy was Alain Blanc I'd think a guy would be positively furious!"

"Not Dave. He trusts me," Tess mused. "Or maybe he just hasn't thought about it. He doesn't seem to take me very seriously lately."

"Are you sure it's all Dave?" Stacy asked.

"Of course I'm sure it's Dave," Tess replied

automatically. The conversation ended as they joined the other girls at the makeup mirror.

"What am I doing, putting on makeup?" Tess exclaimed suddenly, snapping her cosmetics bag closed and throwing it into her purse. "I don't have to look good to drive home and stare at a workbook." She gave a little laugh.

"Can't you come to Nicola's with us?" Gina asked.

"No, I've got too much to do at home," she answered.

"Come for just one quick soda," Stacy urged her. "You'll still get home way before your mom does."

"No, I really can't," she said firmly, turning to go. "What if I started having a really great time and then had to get up and leave? I'd just feel worse. It's easier this way."

"I can understand that," Gina said, and the other girls nodded in agreement. "If you feel like coming over later, Tess, give me a call, okay? We can play Trivial Pursuit or listen to records."

"I'll call if I can," Tess said as she was leaving, "but I've been having a tough time with these new vocabulary words in French class, so I'll probably have my nose in my workbook all night. Thanks for asking, though. See you guys tomorrow!"

As she steered her little Volkswagen through the suburban streets, Tess noticed how many flowers had blossomed in the gardens she passed. Bright red tulips and yellow forsythia brightened the landscape.

Spring has arrived, Tess thought. Most years, Tess reveled in spring, as if she were coming alive after a long winter's hibernation. This year she had barely noticed the changing weather. She was too occupied with questions only time could answer: Would her father forget her completely after he left? Would she pass French? Would she be dropped from cheerleading in her last months of high school? Would she get into Winston or be forced to go to a second-rate secretarial school? Would horrid Paul Holland actually become her stepbrother?

She chuckled humorlessly. No wonder she was looking forward to being tutored. Alain was the only positive development in her life. Her poor grades, her mother's romance, her father's departure, Dave's unpredictable moods weren't anything to look forward to.

Although the afternoon had gone well, even cheerleading wasn't bringing Tess the satisfaction it had in the past. She was too worried about losing her spot on the squad to approach the practice sessions with the same carefree energy as the other girls. With every jump, every kick, a little interior voice asked how many more jumps and kicks she'd be making. Because she wasn't naturally as athletic as most of the others on the squad, Tess approached each game with a slight sense of trepidation. But she was anticipating Saturday's baseball season opener with an anxiety that ran deeper than mere stage fright. If academic probation was in her future, she'd have to make every single game count, cheer for each one as if it were her last.

TWELVE

Tess's mother stopped at home on Wednesday after work just long enough to change into slacks and a casual shirt and to redo her make-up. Then she was off to meet Mr. Holland at his real estate office. Tess was left with an hour and a half before Alain would arrive for their lesson. Mr. Calhoun was dropping him off because Alain didn't think he was ready to try to find his way around Midvale on his own in a borrowed car. Tess had offered to drive him home, hoping he wouldn't be appalled when he saw her battered VW bug.

For dinner, she fixed herself a cold plate of leftover chicken and salad. It wasn't the most satisfying of meals, but she was too tired to prepare anything more complicated.

With less than an hour to dress after she cleared away her dishes, Tess found herself pawing frantically through the contents of her bedroom closet. Alain dressed so well, he plainly cared about fashion. France was the fashion capital of the world. She had to look chic for their first private meeting, without looking as if she'd actually tried to do so.

Her pleated jeans with the snapped ankles were definitely right. But she couldn't decide on a top to go with them. Everything in her dresser and closet was too girlish to wear for an evening with a sophisticated Frenchman. In desperation, she finally headed for her mother's room to explore the racks and drawers there.

Tess was bigger on the bottom than her mother, but they could exchange sweaters and blouses, although they didn't do so frequently. Tess reasoned that this occasion called for an exception.

Her eyes fell almost immediately on the black beaded sweater that was part of a two-piece set. She knew it wasn't the sort of thing her mother would willingly let her borrow. Not that it was expensive or an especial favorite of Mrs. Belding's. But the sweater had a scoop neck and was embellished with scattered black bugle beads.

For the longest time, Tess stared at the sweater in her hands. Then, clutching it, she turned off the light and left the room. Her mother would never have to know about the loan. Tess could drop Alain off, get back home, and change into her sleepshirt before her mother arrived home from the movies.

At seven-twenty, she was ready, and she couldn't have been more pleased with the results. The sweater, jeans, and a pair of black ballet slippers might have come straight from the pages of a French fashion magazine. Deep gray eye shadow and plenty of crayon liner gave Tess's big blue eyes a smoky cast, while the rest of her makeup was muted, just the way her *Makeup Secrets of the Stars* instructed. "'If the eyes are intense,'" Tess recited as she looked in the mirror, "'the other features should be down-played.'" Just to be on the safe side, Tess added an extra coat of black mascara.

She took her French text, workbook, and dictionary downstairs with her, as well as a sheaf of scratch paper. She spread them out across the dining room table, opening the workbook to a half-completed exercise so it would look as if she'd been bent over it most of the evening. Then she poured herself a diet soda and sat down at the table to wait, reading her translation of a passage in the workbook.

"In Paris, the most exciting city in the world," she read, "much of the social life of its inhabitants takes place in the small cafés that line the side streets and the wide boulevards. Here, one can sit and chat with friends for hours over a cup of coffee or a lemonade . . ."

Her thoughts drifted, and the words before her blurred. She saw herself not in the dining area of a townhouse in Clover Farms Estates but beneath the awning of a small sidewalk café on the Left Bank in Paris. A waiter in a white jacket approached, carrying a tray that held frosty glasses of lemonade and a plate of buttery croissants. Across from her at the small marble-topped table sat Alain. "As soon as I saw you in Monsieur Calhoun's homeroom that first day," Alain was telling her, "I knew the time would come when we'd find ourselves in Paris like this . . ."

"You did?" In her fantasy, Tess's tone was confident and teasing, the voice of a girl who knew she was irresistible to all men. "You should have told me right away."

"How could I have done that, *chérie*? I was so intimidated when I saw you. You were so beautiful, so chic, so sure of yourself. I never dreamed I'd ever have the nerve to . . . do this."

He leaned across the small table, one arm reaching to encircle her shoulders and draw her closer to him. His eyes blazed with passion, his lips parted slightly. Tess closed her eyes and waited for his kiss.

A sharp rapping at the door jolted her out of her daze, and she jumped to her feet, the spell broken. She reached up with both hands to fluff her hair as she crossed to the entrance.

"*Bonsoir!*" Alain's hair gleamed like gold in the glow of the porch light.

"Alain! *Bonsoir* . . . hello . . . come in," Tess said, stepping back.

"You are surprised to see me?" he asked as he entered.

"Oh, no. Of course not. I was expecting

you," she stammered. "I, um, was just so involved in studying that the knock at the door startled me. Come sit down." She motioned toward the dining room table. "Would you like a drink?"

"Yes, thank you." He settled into the high-backed chair across from the one she'd been sitting in. "Whatever you are having."

Snap out of it, Belding, she told herself when she was safely hidden in the kitchen. Naturally, she'd looked shocked to see Alain. She couldn't understand at first why he was wearing a Day-Glo orange sweatshirt and camouflage pants instead of the beige linen suit he'd sported in her fantasy.

She left the kitchen and returned to the dining room. "Here you go," she said evenly, setting a tall glass of soda next to Alain before she took her own seat again. Trying to act sophisticated, she asked, "You're not studying any other languages at Midvale, are you?"

"Just English." He grinned. "Mr. Calhoun thought that would be the best for me. At the *lycée*, I also studied Latin and Italian. Spanish I've spoken since I was a small boy. My family has a summer house in Spain," he explained. "Not far from the French border."

"How neat! I can't imagine living in Europe, with so many countries so close together. I'll bet you've done lots of traveling."

"Some," Alain said casually. "I have cousins in the Netherlands my family visits often, and I have been many times to Belgium, Italy, and Germany. And we cross the Channel now and then to shop in London. My father likes British tailoring and has his suits made there. And I like the shops in the Kings Road. This sweatshirt is from England."

"And to think I get excited about going into Chicago to shop," Tess said ruefully. "Illinois isn't close to any other country but Canada. We went there once when I was just a kid. I was excited for weeks. And you know what? It was just like Illinois!"

"But not all of America is like your state, is it?" Alain asked. "I've read much about deserts in the west and the tropical beaches of the south. I hope to travel around the country for a month or so before I return to France. There is so much to see in *les États-Unis*."

"Well, I sure haven't seen a lot of it," Tess admitted. Then, afraid Alain would dismiss her as a hick, she added, "Of course, I'll probably be flying out to California this summer now that my father's moving there."

"Your father, he does not—doesn't—live with you?"

"My folks are divorced," Tess told him. "You must know by now that divorce is one of the great American pastimes. My mother and father split up last year, and now that the divorce is final he's moving to Los Angeles," she added blithely.

"I am sorry your parents are no longer

married," Alain said seriously. "How lucky it doesn't seem to bother you. And now you will get to go to California, eh? I plan to stop there on my touring. I would like to see the film studios in Hollywood and the Golden Gate Bridge in San Francisco."

"Maybe we'll be in L.A. at the same time!" Tess said as the thought occurred to her. "Wouldn't that be fun?"

"That would be very nice," Alain agreed mildly. "Perhaps I should look at those." He motioned toward her French books.

"Oh, sure," Tess agreed. But it was hard to conceal her disappointment as she pushed the books across the table. She'd much rather talk about Alain and his life in Paris than have to work on her grueling French exercises. But he was going to be strictly businesslike.

Tess scolded herself as she realized what she was thinking. Nothing was more important than mastering French.

Alain proved to be an excellent tutor. He was patient and understanding, and not once, not even when she made ridiculous mistakes in verb conjugations, did he laugh or treat her like anything but a very intelligent person. Meanwhile, Tess tried earnestly to prove to Alain that she wasn't a hopeless student. Luckily, they were reviewing the last few chapters that had been covered in class, so she was familiar with the work.

When they agreed to call it quits at nine-thirty, she leaned back in her chair with a pleased smile. "You should be a teacher!" she complimented him. "Do you know, I think I understand the subjunctive now for the first time ever? What would I do without you?"

Alain chuckled, shaking his head modestly. "It is not me who is doing all the work, Tess. It is you. You know all the basics of the language—now you just need some help in putting the pieces together, like a game. A puzzle."

"Speaking of games, how did you like playing American baseball in phys ed?" she asked.

"I like it very much," he answered in his straightforward way. "It is a little bit like our lacrosse. But there is something very American about standing with a big wooden bat in your hands. It made me feel like a real Yankee!"

"Wait till you see the game on Saturday. You'll be impressed by some of our players," she promised.

He nodded. "One of them was in that class with me. Rich Stinson?"

Tess nodded back. "He's a great athlete," she said. "His girlfriend's on the cheering squad with me—Kathy Phillips. She's a year behind us."

"And another boy on the baseball team—Dave Prentice—he is your boyfriend, *non*? He takes the same physics class as I do. He seems like a—how do you say?—good guy."

"He's very nice," Tess said simply. "You seem to have met quite a few kids already."

Alain's face lit up. "It is so easy here in America," he said. "Everyone is very open, very friendly. Rich has offered to drive me around and show me the sights sometime. Of course, he is very busy right now with athletics. He says many different colleges have offered him athletic scholarships. So much money they give to sports stars in America! *C'est incroyable!* Truly incredible."

"I guess Rich must have a lot on his mind these days with his last season at Midvale just gearing up," Tess commented. "It's a shame he may not have the time to show you around."

"Well, I guess I'll just have to do my sightseeing with someone else," Alain said philosophically. He went on, "This is what I mean about Americans being so friendly—Rich is not the only one who made the gesture. You know a girl named Valerie? A very pretty girl with very long blond hair? She has promised to drive me into Chicago to show me what she calls the Loop and the famous Art Institute."

"You must mean Valerie Masters," Tess said. "I *suppose* she's pretty, and she *is* blond. Do you like blonds?" she asked innocently. "I thought opposites were supposed to attract."

He smiled coyly back at her. "I like all kinds of women. Of course," he added slowly, "I've always preferred brunettes and redheads myself but"—his smile turned sad and he shrugged broadly—"sometimes a man has to make compromises. If his first choice isn't available . . ."

Tess waited for him to finish his sentence. When he didn't, she ducked her head to hide the confusion and pleasure on her face. Alain was flirting with her! He seemed to be asking just how serious she and Dave were about each other. When she'd collected herself, she raised her head to meet his eyes. "I don't think you'll be able to convince Valerie to dye her hair," she said. "It's her pride and joy."

"She probably believes that all gentlemen prefer blonds," Alain remarked. There was an intimacy in his tone as he added, "But I don't think that is true. Do you?"

"I hope not," Tess purred, enjoying Alain's outright admiration. "How do you say in French: 'to each his own'?"

"*Chacun à son goût*," Alain replied. "'Each to his own taste.'" Looking down at his watch, he sighed. "Although it is *not* to my taste, I should go back to the Calhouns' house now. I think I am going to have to do more studying than I expected, especially in physics. I find it difficult to understand so much technical material in English."

"Let me know if I can help," Tess offered.

"I can think of lots of ways you could help," Alain told her, smiling sexily, "but none of them has to do with physics." He laughed as she looked away, flustered. "I hope I can tease with you, Tess. I sense that you have much spirit,

110

much of what we call *joie de vivre*—joy of living. Dennis Callahan said he'd be glad to translate any physics terms I had trouble with."

"Oh, good." Tess jumped to her feet, unsure how to respond to Alain's personal comments. "I just have to grab my jacket and then we can get going. My car heater isn't the best, so I hope you don't freeze. It still gets nippy after the sun goes down."

"I like the cold weather," Alain told her as they were leaving. "In the winter, my cousin Yves and I go skiing with his father, my uncle Gaston. He has a small chalet in the Swiss Alps."

"Switzerland! See, there's another country you've been to that I've only dreamed about," Tess said as she led Alain across the parking lot to her car.

"This is your car?" he asked as she unlocked the door for him, and Tess had a momentary qualm. Alain was probably used to riding in sleek European sports cars.

But when she nodded, he simply said, "I like these cars. Uncle Gaston keeps a Volkswagen at his chalet because it climbs the steep roads so well."

"It doesn't look like much, but it gets me where I'm going," Tess told him. Then, as she turned the key in the ignition and the engine exploded into life with a loud backfire, she laughed. "I guess it doesn't *sound* like much, either." She shifted into reverse and backed out of the space.

"I hope I was of some help to you," Alain said a few minutes later after she'd pulled to the curb by the Calhouns' house. It was on Marshall Road, not far from where Gina Damone lived.

"Oh, you were," Tess assured him. "You were a huge help! I'm already feeling more confident about passing the midterm."

"After a few more lessons, we must start working on conversational French instead of using the textbook," Alain suggested. "With the text, we just read and talk about life in Paris, and I already know about that. I want to hear all about *you*."

"I promise I'll tell all," Tess drawled. It was much easier to flirt in the darkness of the car. "After all, you're the tutor. You get to make the rules."

As she drove off, she replayed the evening in her mind. Frenchmen obviously did have a way with women. Somehow Alain had managed to make it seem almost as if Tess were doing him a favor by letting him tutor her. And when he'd said it was time for him to leave, he'd sounded genuinely regretful.

Only one innocent comment Alain had made marred Tess's recollection of the evening: he'd said that people—like Rich and Dennis and Valerie—were offering to show him around.

Tess liked Rich. She had thought Stacy was crazy when she'd broken up with him in the fall.

And she didn't think Rich or somebody like Dennis Callahan would cause Alain to abandon his tutoring sessions with her.

But Valerie Masters was a potential problem.

Tess wouldn't have been surprised to learn that Valerie planned to befriend Alain just to influence his opinion of Tess. Tess resolved to watch Val closely—and to make sure Alain got tuned in to Val's nasty ways very early.

Alain didn't even notice my slinky sweater, she thought with a sigh. *Or, if he did, he didn't comment on it.* Remembering that she was still wearing the black top, Tess pressed her foot a little harder on the accelerator. She could worry about Alain later. For the time being, she had to get the sweater back in her mother's closet before her mother came home and found her wearing it. The clock on the dashboard showed ten o'clock. Tess wished for the first time that her mother and Burt would have such a good time they'd stay out late just this once.

THIRTEEN

All day Thursday, Tess mused that Burt Holland might not be such a bad addition to her mother's life. He hadn't brought her mother home until after the black sweater had been returned safely to her mother's closet. There might be other times when it would be best if her mother wasn't hanging around the house, and Mr. Holland would certainly be helpful then.

But by Thursday night, she wished once again that her mother had never met the man. That was when her mother announced that the Hollands would be coming to dinner on Friday evening. "But, Mom," Tess protested, "you know Dave and I always do something on Fridays!"

"You've both got to eat, no matter what you do later on," her mother reminded her. "I thought Dave could join us, too."

"Great," Tess muttered, but she dutifully invited Dave. At least she wouldn't have to suffer alone through stories about Burt Holland's college football career or Paul's latest home-improvement project.

"I'm sure it's going to be a great big drag," Tess groaned when she called Dave, "but there's no way I can get out of it, and Mom would really like you to come."

"That sounds terrific," Dave said enthusiastically. "My dad knows Burt Holland and says he's a great guy. It should be a lot of fun with Paul along. It'll be sort of like dinner theater—free food and free comedy."

"I guess," Tess agreed listlessly. But when she hung up, she was angry with Dave all over again. He acted pleased that he wouldn't have to spend the evening alone with her—even though the alternative was to spend it with Paul Holland.

Tess's annoyance about the dinner distracted her all day Friday. For the first time ever, she scored less than 90 words per minute during shorthand practice. In word processing workshop, she had to ask the teacher for her computer password, which she had forgotten, even though she'd been using it every day since the beginning of the school year.

The pep rally was a personal flop. First Tess forgot the words to "Bases Are Loaded," an old standby cheer. Then her solo back jump, performed with the eyes of the entire student body on her alone, was sloppy and second-rate. Her back was almost straight instead of fully arched, and her feet leaned to the right when they should have been tucked neatly beneath her. If she had been at tryouts instead of a pep rally, she wouldn't have made the squad.

In the locker room afterward, Gina told everyone, "Good rally, gang," singling Tess out for a sympathetic smile. But Tess was in no mood to be humored.

"Are you kidding?" she snorted in disgust. "It was the absolute pits!" She grabbed her jacket and books and stormed out without another word.

When she got home, an envelope from Winston was waiting for her. Inside were forms for her final application as well as a notice that Midvale High had been requested to forward Tess's transcripts as soon as her final grades were available. Tess tossed the envelope on the dining room sideboard in despair. Not only was she going to flunk French; at this rate, she wouldn't pass typing. She had been dreaming to think she was good enough to get into Winston in the first place.

When her dad called to remind her about Sunday's brunch, she purposely cut the conversation short. She wanted to cancel their date, but she knew she might regret it when her father was gone, even if he was only seeing her out of obligation.

Dinner, of course, was a disaster.

It started badly when Tess carelessly dumped so much vinegar in the salad dressing that Mr. Holland almost choked on it. Mrs. Belding had rushed in embarrassment to the kitchen for more olive oil to repair the dressing as much as possible. Tess felt bad for her mother but was silent.

Paul, however, was happy to fill in the gaps in conversation, especially with a popular senior boy like Dave Prentice in his audience.

"You should have seen Tess at the rally, Dad," he said several times. "She's really a great cheerleader!" It was almost as if he wanted to remind her of her bad performance. Tess just smiled wanly each time. In an effort to impress Dave, Paul talked about sports, describing in detail several of Dave's plays of the basketball season. "I wish I weren't such a runt," he told Dave in a voice that affected Tess like fingernails scraping on a blackboard. "I'd love to be good at basketball. Or any sports, come to think of it."

"We can't all be superathletes, Paul," his father told him. *As if Paul could even aspire to be average*, Tess thought. "I wasn't much good at basketball myself. Too brawny, I suppose." He winked at Mrs. Belding. "Of course, back then I carried the weight in my shoulders and not at my belt."

Tess was beginning to feel the heat of her mother's sideward glances, urging her to participate in the conversation. "You're not the least bit fat," she told Mr. Holland. "I think you're in good shape for somebody your age."

"Tess!" her mother exclaimed with a laugh.

"We're not exactly doddering yet!" They all laughed at her then—Dave included—and Tess resolved to say as little as possible for the rest of the meal.

Not even Dave seemed to notice her unhappiness. He was too busy encouraging Paul to chatter and brag. "Hear you took early SATs and got almost perfect scores," he told Paul.

"They weren't that great," Paul insisted, then quoted his scores.

"That's better than I did on two tries," Dave told him. "I guess grades are more important than sports in the long run!"

"I think that's the way it should be," Mr. Holland said. "A sports scholarship means you've got all sorts of pressure on you, without much time to work on your studies. Unless a guy's good enough to turn pro, all the sports in the world aren't going to make him a success in the outside world. Then he's left with a weak academic background when he tries to get a job."

"That makes sense," Dave agreed. "I guess I really think of sports as a hobby."

"Me, too," said Tess, "which is a good thing, since I don't suppose there are many cheerleading jobs around out there for middle-aged women."

Dave glared at her, but Paul snatched the chance to make one of his corny jokes. "I never heard of a Dallas Cowgrandmother, did you?"

Even Mrs. Belding laughed at that crack. Tess simply smiled stiffly.

Tess sighed in relief when her mother asked her to help clear the dishes. At last, she and Dave could escape. But when she returned from her first trip to the kitchen, Dave thanked her mother and said good night. Without even asking Tess to walk with him to his car, he grabbed his coat and was gone. Tess didn't protest. She refused to beg him for his company in front of everyone.

Her mother left with the Hollands soon afterward, leaving Tess with the dinner dishes to clean before she went to bed. She loaded the dishwasher, stuck the leftovers in the fridge, and was upstairs in bed by nine-thirty. She cried herself to sleep, taking comfort only in the thought that at least her life couldn't get much worse.

Tess awoke Saturday with the memory of the previous evening fresh in her mind. The prospect of cheering was usually enough to raise her spirits, no matter how glum she felt. But today she dreaded facing the team and the fans with a big smile on her face, acting as if she hadn't a care in the world. *But that's exactly what I'm going to do*, she determined. *Boys like Dave Prentice and Paul Holland aren't going to spoil everything for me!*

After she dressed, Tess spent the morning cleaning her room. She slid the window open so the fresh, crisp spring air could waft in through the screens while she stripped her bed and remade it with fresh linens. Then she fixed a light lunch and took it to the sunny dining room to eat. By the time her mother emerged from her bedroom it was close to noon, and the warm spring air and hard work had put Tess in much better spirits.

"Having a late breakfast, dear?" Mrs. Belding asked as she headed into the kitchen to start a pot of coffee.

Tess rolled her eyes, even though she knew her mother couldn't see from the other room. "No, this is—" She paused, then asked innocently, "Now, what is it they call a late brunch? Lunch! That's it. This is lunch."

"If I didn't know you better, I'd say you were making fun of me." Mrs. Belding chuckled as she took a seat opposite Tess, a glass of orange juice in her hand. "What's that you're eating?"

"Tuna on diet bread. With a game at two, I didn't want to have anything too heavy."

"Mmmm, smell that coffee!" Mrs. Belding inhaled deeply as the coffee maker started sputtering and chugging in the kitchen.

"Out late?" Tess asked, finishing the rest of the sandwich and sipping her diet soda.

"Too late," her mother groaned. "I can't believe I slept till noon. And I've still got to do all the grocery shopping, gas up the car, hit the dry cleaner's, and run out to the mall to pick up panty hose and get new lifts put on my taupe shoes. The working woman's life ain't an easy one," she added with a rueful smile.

"What did you guys do last night, anyway?"

To Tess's surprise, her mother giggled like a young girl. "After we took Paul home, Burt suggested we go have a drink someplace. We ended up dancing until the place closed—at Jiminy's, out on the highway."

"Jiminy's!" Tess almost choked on her soda. "Mom, that's a college hangout! A rock-and-roll club!"

"Well, I remind you again that neither Burt nor I is a senior citizen," her mother retorted, still smiling. "You should see him dance! They did a whole hour of oldies, and he knew every single dance we did back in high school and junior high. The Mashed Potato and the Jerk and the Hully Gully—"

"But do *you* know how to do all those things?" Tess was flabbergasted.

"I just lived for dancing from the time I was thirteen," her mother told her, a faraway look in her eyes. "My biggest dream when I was a kid was to win an appearance on Bandstand and a trip to Philadelphia."

"*You?* I can't believe it." Tess shook her head, still stunned. "I never knew you liked to dance, Mom. I mean, I know you love the Beatles and the Rolling Stones—"

"I was already married by the time those groups got really famous," her mother reminisced. "Your father was majoring in accounting at the University of Illinois, and we had a little apartment off-campus in Urbana. He used to like the Beatles and Stones, too, in those days, if you can believe it. But he never did like to dance. I think last night was the first time I've rocked and rolled since my tenth high-school reunion. And even then I had to get somebody else to dance with me because your father thought it wasn't dignified!" She chuckled.

Tess nodded. "I can't picture Dad letting go," she admitted.

"You should have seen Burt!" Her mother's eyes sparkled with excitement. "Even some of those kids were impressed."

"Didn't you feel funny, though? Being with all those college kids."

"Not in the least. As long as you're having a good time, nobody cares how old you are. Anyhow, there were several other couples there at least as old as us." She stood up as the coffee maker lapsed into silence. "Coffee's done," she said, turning toward the kitchen. Then she groaned and rubbed her hip. "I forgot dancing's exercise. I feel like I had a real workout last night."

As Tess headed upstairs to shower and change into her cheerleading uniform, she was still shaking her head. She heard her mother whistling a Beatles tune as she fixed herself a cup of coffee and a bite to eat in the kitchen. That meant she was happy indeed.

Tess had just finished drying her hair and doing her makeup when her mother tapped at the bathroom door. "I'm off to do my errands," she said when Tess opened it. "Got any dry cleaning you need done?"

"Oh, could you take my tan slacks in? They're on the chair in my room."

"Will do. Will you be home after the game?"

Tess shook her head. "Stacy's having everybody over to her house afterward, so I suppose I'll eat there. What are you up to?"

Tess was sure her mother was blushing. "Burt's going to the game with Paul and one of Paul's friends," she said. "Then we're all going bowling out at Bowlarama."

"Bowling? Don't tell me you know how to bowl, too!"

"Nope, but Burt's going to show me how. Good luck at the game, sweetie!"

Lately, Tess thought, *Mom is a constant surprise.* She glanced at her watch. She had a half hour before she had to leave to pick up Gina. She collected her makeup and repaired the damage she'd done to the bathroom, then wandered downstairs to the living room.

She flopped onto the couch and flipped through the magazine rack standing at its end. The latest issue of *Cosmopolitan* caught her eye immediately. "The French Man," one of its cover titles read. "Are You Woman Enough for Him?"

Tess turned to the article. There was a

picture of a guy who looked like an older version of Alain, in a black turtleneck and black leather pants. *This might be interesting*, she told herself. She stretched out on the couch and began to read.

FOURTEEN

Tess tugged nervously at a lock of curly hair as the Mustangs took their position on the field. Midvale had finished the eighth inning leading by just one run. Carson would be at bat first in the ninth.

"Brrr!" Stacy hugged her arms around herself as the cheerleaders huddled together for warmth. "It's starting to get cold now that the sun's going down."

"Those Carson cheerleaders can't be keeping warm just standing around like that," Patricia said scornfully, gesturing toward the six girls leading cheers in front of the rival team's bleachers. "They're even lazier now than they were during basketball season."

"Too bad their baseball team isn't so lazy," Gina said. "They've still got a chance. A seven-to-six score doesn't give us much of an edge for the last inning in the game."

"Well, let's give the boys a last-inning cheer that'll keep us ahead. What do you think?" Stacy turned to Gina. "Should we do 'When the Mustangs Come to Bat' before the inning starts?"

Gina gave it her okay. "And we'll do 'Strike Him Out' while Carson's at bat. And a special cheer for Rich if he's pitching again."

Tess was eyeing the rival cheerleaders as they finished their cheer with lackluster jumps, pom-poms hanging limply at their sides. "I should have gone to Carson," she cracked. "Then I'd be the best cheerleader on the squad!"

"Oh, no!" Stacy squealed in mock horror. "What would we do without you, Tess?"

"The same as you do with me. Grin and bear it!"

"Come on." Stacy gave Tess a playful punch on the arm. "Let's go strut our stuff."

The girls lined up at the front of the home team's bleachers. Dave walked by on his way to the field, but he was unaware of Tess. His forehead was creased in concentration and his shoulders were set. The coach wouldn't let the players get too smug when they were leading by such a slim margin.

As the squad started their cheer, swooping low with their pom-poms in a locomotion roll, Tess stole a glance at the dugout. She was glad to see the Carson team looking worried. Midvale was bound to win!

The cheer they were doing was a long one, almost more a dance routine. Tess managed to keep smiling and to remember the words as she followed Stacy and Gina through the complicated choreography: two mule kicks, a right side leap, a long ripple with the pom-poms, left side leap. She was warm from exertion in spite of the fact that the sun was low on the horizon. The Midvale fielders were in place as the girls recited the last line to the cheer.

"Yep, we're gonna show you where it's at,
     When Midvale comes to bat!"

Back jumps in unison marked the end of the cheer, with a final pom-pom ripple after the girls had landed.

Over the din of the applauding crowd, Tess could hear one voice screeching, "Ya, Tess! Show 'em, Tess!" Just as the lights went on all over the field, she spied her booster. It was Paul Holland, sitting in the front row with his father. She pretended she didn't see them as she walked to the cheerleaders' bench to catch her breath.

The first batter had a full count—three balls and two strikes—before Rich finally struck him out. The Midvale stands went wild. Tess cheered with them, surprised at the pained expression on Gina's face when she looked at her.

"You're tense," Tess told her. "Are you that cold?"

"Worried," Gina said flatly. "It looks like Rich is winding down."

Sure enough, as the second batter took his place in the batter's box, Rich's shoulders seemed to slump. He pitched a strike immediately, but on the second pitch, the batter hit a hard grounder and made it to first base.

"C'mon," Stacy said quickly, "we'd better be on our feet for this one."

As they ran to take their places in front of the stands, the girls were already chanting, "Strike him out, strike him out, give us an out!"

But the third batter walked, putting men on first and second bases for Carson.

The fourth man up hit a high fly ball to short left field, an easy catch. The second out.

Tess could almost feel the tension growing in both sets of bleachers. One more out, and it was all over, the Mustangs' game.

Instead, the fifth batter got a base hit, advancing the two other runners to second and third base.

"Uh-oh," Gina muttered in Tess's ear. "Now it's nail-biting time."

Rich's first pitch was high and wide to the left. Ball one.

The second pitch crossed the corner of the plate by a hair, just enough to make it a strike. "Way to go, Stinson!" the cheerleaders yelled.

The third pitch was low. Ball two. A collective gasp rose from the Midvale bleachers. If Rich walked this batter, Carson would score a run and the bases would still be loaded.

And then it happened. Rich pitched a curve ball that should have been ball three, since it looked as if it would go far wide of the plate. But the batter leaned into the pitch when he saw it coming. The ball and the bat connected with the sharp rifle crack of wood on leather, and the ball was gone. It was a home run, out of the ballpark. A grand slam, four runs scored for Carson.

"Yikes!" Even Stacy lost her cool and was frantically running her fingers through her hair. "We're in trouble now."

The Midvale stands were quiet, the Carson fans went crazy, and Midvale's coach called for a time-out. Tess's stomach turned as she watched the scoreboard numbers flipping to show the new score. Ten to seven, Carson leading.

"You think the coach is taking Rich out?" Kathy's pretty face was twisted with pain.

Gina shook her head. "I think he's trying to assure him it wasn't his fault. He won't take Rich out of the game now unless Rich insists he's too tired to finish out the inning. That was a ball. Who'd have thought anybody would go for it and turn it into a grand-slam homer?"

"Good, he's staying in!" Kathy heaved a sigh of relief as the Midvale coach left the field and the next Carson batter stepped up to the plate.

"Let's just hope Rich gets that third out— and fast!" Tess muttered.

She didn't have to worry. Rich struck the next batter out before he even had a chance to swing his bat.

"Now it's up to Midvale," Stacy said dramatically. "We either sink or swim."

Never had time seemed to pass as slowly as it did during the bottom half of the ninth inning. Carson's pitcher struck out the first Mustang at bat. Rich Stinson was second in the batting order, and he bunted and made it to first base as the Midvale crowds cheered him like a hero.

The next Midvale man up was taken out at first on a grounder, but Rich made it to second base.

The cheerleaders stood in a tight line, clutching one another's hands, as Dave Prentice came to the plate. It was almost dark, and Dave looked pale in the harsh gleam of the artificial light. The bleachers were so quiet they might have been empty.

Three balls, and the tension was unbearable. Then the pitcher let loose with a fast ball aimed straight across the middle of the plate. Dave connected too low on the bat. The ball soared in the air and fell with a plop into the first baseman's glove as he jogged in.

"That's all, folks," Stacy said ruefully, scuffling the toe of her sneaker in the turf. "Guess I'm going to be having a wake and not a party."

"Bummer!" Patricia tossed her head and looked indignantly over to where the Carson cheering squad were hugging each other and jumping for joy. "They didn't deserve to win, not with those lame cheerleaders."

"It isn't whether you win or lose, it's how you play the game," Sherri said philosophically. "And our guys did a great job. First we cheered for them, and now we're going to have to cheer them up."

"Right," Gina said firmly as she started gathering up pom-poms and their other gear. "Put smiles on your faces for the party, gang. We may be losers now, but we've all got to feel like winners by the time we get to Stacy's."

Tess had grabbed her things and was about to follow the other girls inside to the locker room when she heard what was becoming an all too familiar voice calling her name. She kept going as if she hadn't heard. Then she remembered that Mr. Holland was with his son. Her mother would never forgive her if she was rude to Burt Holland.

She stopped and turned. "Hi, Paul. Hi, Mr. Holland. Not Midvale's greatest game, was it?"

"I've seen lots worse," Burt Holland said. "The home team played a fine game. Anyone as active as I was in high-school athletics knows that some you lose and some you win."

"And never the twain shall meet!" Paul cut in, rolling his eyes so wildly Tess was afraid his lenses might pop out.

She laughed in spite of herself. "At least it's the first game of the season and not the last," she said.

"Carson's not so hot," Paul insisted aggressively. "And their cheerleaders are for the birds. What a pathetic bunch! I've seen more energy in a rock garden!"

"I hope we looked better than they did," Tess said.

"Are you kidding?" Paul nearly yelled. "The Mustangs have the best cheering squad in the district! And you're right up there with the best of them, Tess. Even Dad said so, didn't you?"

Burt Holland nodded. "You've got so much pep, you'd be a millionairess if you could bottle it and put it up for sale."

"Thanks for the compliment," Tess said. "I'm not on the same level as girls like Gina and Sherri, but I try my best."

"They may be the best at the jumps and leaps and all that." Paul seemed determined not to drop the subject. "But you've got something special, Tess. The way you cheer—everyone can see it's really important to you and that you really believe Midvale's the best. That counts for a lot."

"Midvale really *is* the best," Tess said.

The three of them stood silently for a few seconds. Paul was fidgeting—Tess saw him raise one hand to his mouth, before he caught himself and stopped.

"Well, we'd better get a move on," Mr. Holland finally said. "Did your mom tell you we're all going bowling? We wish you could come along, Tess." He turned to his son before Tess could respond. "Where did Jason get to, Paul?"

Paul looked around, then said, "He's over

there in back of the bleachers talking to some girl."

Following his glance, Tess was startled to see that the Jason in question was Jason Phelps. It surprised her that a popular boy like Jason would go to the game and be going bowling with Paul Holland. To Mr. Holland, she said, "Watch out for my mother. I've got a feeling a bowling ball could become a lethal weapon in her hands!"

"Will do." He chuckled.

"And don't tell her I warned you," Tess called after them.

Then she turned and hurried across the dark field to the gym.

FIFTEEN

By the time she got to Stacy's house, Haw-thorne Lane was already clogged with cars, and Tess had to park almost a block away. The big white house was brightly lit. From the backyard came the smoky scent of grilled hot dogs and burgers. Tess followed her nose.

Alexander Harcourt was standing in front of the big built-in gas grill at the end of the patio, flanked by Dennis Callahan and Jeremy. "Is this the KP department?" Tess asked. As the three greeted her, Tess thought, *Only Stacy's father could manage to look distinguished wearing a denim apron and holding a long spatula in one hand.*

"The gang's downstairs," he told her. "We're just dishing up the first round of food for anyone who's too hungry to wait another min-ute."

"Better get inside if you want any potato salad," Jeremy chimed in. "Stinson's already gone through half the bowl!"

"He must have worked up some appetite on

the mound today," Tess said as she opened the screened back door.

The noise of loud music and at least twenty people talking at once poured up the stairs that led to the Harcourts' huge lower-level rec room. When Tess reached the bottom of the stairs, she saw that practically everyone she'd expected to find was already there.

Rich Stinson was standing by the long table that held bowls and plates overflowing with food, and Tess walked over to him first. "Good game, Rich," she said warmly. "You really played your heart out today."

"Thanks, Tess." He smiled, but Tess could tell he was trying not to show how hard he took this defeat. "I think all the guys did a great job."

Next to him, Kathy stood and massaged the shoulder of his pitching arm. "Just wait," she said with feeling. "We'll whop Carson the next time around."

"I've got to find a cold drink. I'm dying of thirst," Tess told them, heading over to the built-in wet bar where she'd already spotted Dave surrounded by a group that included Stacy, Gina, and Tony.

It wasn't until she was almost on top of them that Tess spied Valerie Masters. If only Stacy hadn't invited her! But it wouldn't do to snub the head majorette at a post-game celebration. Not that there was much to celebrate tonight.

"There's Tess now," Stacy said as she approached.

"We were starting to wonder if you were going to show up," Gina told her with a smile of welcome.

"Valerie said she saw you going off with Paul Holland and his dad," Dave told her.

"I was hardly going off with them," Tess corrected Dave, doing her best to ignore Valerie. "They just stopped me to talk for a minute." She turned to Stacy. "Got a diet soda back there someplace?"

As Stacy poured her drink, Tess fumed. It was one thing for Valerie to spy on her—she expected that sort of low behavior from her—but did Dave have to parrot Val's lies in front of everyone?

"Don't let me interrupt your conversation," she trilled in a high, unnatural voice.

"Don't worry," Tony assured her, "we needed a new topic of conversation. Everybody was rehashing the game for me, to fill me in on what I missed. Not the most pleasant subject in the world."

Tess shrugged. "Midvale did a job nobody should be ashamed of," she said staunchly.

"We still lost," Dave cut in bluntly, his expression grim.

"But look how close we came to winning," Tess argued. "Midvale showed it's got one of the best baseball teams around. Losing a game in the last inning is better than losing it from the start, right?"

"Not when you're the one who lost it," Dave said quietly.

"Somebody had to be the one to get the last out," Tess said matter-of-factly, trying to cheer him up.

But instead of looking gratified, Dave glared at her as if she'd insulted him. But Tess was in no mood for a fight, especially not in front of Valerie and the others, so she decided to switch the subject. "Their cheerleaders sure weren't much, were they?" she asked brightly.

Dave snorted. "That's much more important than how our team did, isn't it?" he asked, his voice tight. Then he shrugged. "Think I'll go get one of those burgers Jeremy's bringing in."

There was an awkward silence as he moved away, broken by Valerie Masters's drawl. "Oh, dear, Joanie's discovered that plate of brownies! I'd better grab one before they disappear."

"Boy!" Tess exploded when Valerie had walked away. "Dave's sure a barrel of laughs tonight, isn't he?"

"He's taking the loss pretty hard," Gina said gently. "I suppose it's easy for him to blame himself, since he was last at bat."

"But he knows better than to think it was all his fault," Tess argued. "It's silly of him to take the blame."

"The guy's upset," Tony reminded her. "You can't expect him to be rational."

137

"Can't I expect him to be polite, either?" Tess asked, her voice shaking. "I can't believe he just stormed away from me like that!"

"He'll cool off," Stacy predicted. "Just make sure you let him see you're on his side."

Tess sighed. If Dave expected to be babied, she was definitely going to give him time to calm down before she tried to talk to him again. It wasn't fair of Dave to ruin the party for her because he was in a rotten mood. "How did your game go, Tony?" she asked.

"We won. Knocked 'em off the field. Of course," he confessed with a dimpled grin, "we were up against the worst team in the whole district, so there wasn't much of a contest."

Tess talked to Gina and Tony for a half hour, then excused herself to get a hamburger. She couldn't find Dave anywhere, but she heard voices coming from around the corner of the L-shaped room, so she took her plate in that direction.

The first thing she saw was the pool table, where Dex had just racked the balls for a game with Alain Blanc. Tess hadn't noticed Alain in the stands earlier. Now she wondered how she could have missed him. He was wearing black jeans and a green sweater. As soon as he saw her enter the room, Alain smiled warmly.

"Dex insists only Americans can be pool sharks," he called to her. "I'm going to show him he's wrong."

Tess's own smile disappeared as she saw

Dave and Valerie Masters sharing a couch, talking as if they were alone in the room.

Dave spotted her then and gestured for her to join them. "There's room for one more here!"

She shook her head. He knew how she felt about Val! "I'll have a whole sofa to myself over there," she said coolly, then crossed to the other side of the room and took a seat on the long couch behind the pool table.

Dave said nothing and remained sitting with Valerie, again talking as if Tess had never arrived. But Tess kept a smile on her face and concentrated on her burger.

When Alain cleared the table, winning handily over Dex Grantham, Tess cheered him loudly. "What do you think?" he asked as he came over to join her on the couch. "Can Frenchmen shoot pool as well as Americans?"

"Mais oui!" she joked, laughing merrily, but her eyes were on Dave. If he cared that she was flirting with another boy, it didn't show. But she could play his game. "How are you enjoying the party?" she asked Alain.

"It's very nice," Alain answered seriously. "I ate too much, though. So much food, and all so good!"

"Not very French, though, is it?" Tess asked.

"No," he admitted, "but in Paris, we love American-style hamburgers. Every weekend night, there are lines a block long outside such restaurants."

"Really?" Tess laughed gaily. "The more I hear about Paris, the crazier it sounds. I can't wait to go there." Impetuously, she took his hand. "Now, come and work off some of those calories! You can prove to me that Frenchmen are better dancers than Americans, too!"

As Tess expected, Alain was a great dancer. His dancing was less stiff and jerky than the movements of the local boys. And he was really a dancing partner, not just the guy across from her on the floor. Alain kept his eyes on Tess, and he danced so close that their bodies were touching more than they were apart. The other boys looked silly next to Alain. They might have been by themselves on the floor, but Alain was clearly with her.

"Where did you ever learn to dance like that?" she asked when the music stopped, determined not to let Alain slip away from her. She wanted Dave to see she was getting plenty of attention without him.

"The discos," he told her. "France doesn't have too many good rock bands, but we all love the American and British music. At home I go dancing every week."

"With a different girl every time?" Tess asked, lowering her lashes flirtatiously.

"Sometimes," he admitted. "But only because the girls I know in Paris don't dance as well as you do."

"Let's get something cold to drink," Tess suggested.

Alain poured two glasses of ginger ale and handed one to Tess.

"Champagne?" she asked with feigned innocence.

"What else would a Frenchman give to a girl he was trying to impress?" he answered, his eyes twinkling.

"To France!" Tess toasted, holding her glass high.

"To America," Alain answered, "and to American girls."

"All American girls?" Tess asked as she clinked her glass against his.

"I don't know them all," Alain answered lightly, sipping his drink. "But if they are all like the one I know the best, they're *fantastique!*"

It was easy for Tess to mingle at the party with Alain by her side. He naturally attracted attention. Alain was as casually flirtatious as the *Cosmo* article predicted. But he couldn't take Tess's mind off Dave. She refused to be caught searching for him, but all she really wanted was for him to come and insist that she join him and leave Alain behind.

"I must say good night," Alain finally said. "Rich is giving me a ride home, and he and Kathy are leaving now."

"I had no idea it was so late!" Tess jumped to her feet. "I'm going to get one more soda and hit the road myself," she said.

"What time should I come by tomorrow?" Alain asked.

"Better make it about four, if that's all right," Tess said. She was having brunch with her father earlier. As Alain nodded, she asked, "Want me to pick you up?"

"Thank you, but I've decided to try driving on my own. Since it will be daylight, I should be all right."

Alain went off with Rich and Kathy, and Tess started looking for Dave. She was astonished when she couldn't find him anywhere. She looked in the main room, the pool-table room, and even out back on the patio. But he was nowhere to be seen.

Finally, she found Stacy, who was in the kitchen with Jeremy, the two of them standing over an ice cream carton, digging into it with spoons.

"Ah-hah, caught in the act!"

Jeremy stopped, his spoon in midair on the way to his mouth. "Uh-oh!" He looked at Stacy solemnly. "Now what are we going to do? Tess knows our deep dark secret."

"I think we can trust her," Stacy assured him. Tess could tell she was having a hard time keeping a straight face. "Especially if we give her a spoon and tell her to dig in."

"Thanks, but I'm really not hungry," Tess admitted. "I was looking for Dave. Have you seen him?"

Stacy and Jeremy exchanged a look before Stacy asked slowly, "You mean he didn't tell you he was leaving?"

"If he had, I wouldn't be looking for him, would I? When did he go?"

"Long time ago," Jeremy answered. "Maybe an hour, hour and a half."

Tess swallowed hard. "You mean he just walked out?"

"He said goodbye to us," Stacy said uncertainly. "He took losing the game really hard, Tess. I think he was just going home to crash."

Gritting her teeth, Tess forced herself to smile. "Guess I was having such a good time he didn't want to interrupt me to say good night," she said brightly. "He'll probably call me the minute I get home, if he's not trying to call right now."

"Tess, maybe you should give *him* a ring," Stacy suggested. "I think he was feeling pretty low."

Tess continued to smile brightly. "We all have our bad days, don't we? I'd better get home myself. Better get that spoon in your mouth, Jeremy," she added as she turned away. "That ice cream's going to drip all over your sweater."

"Tess—"

Tess didn't wait to find out what Stacy wanted to say. All she wanted right that minute was to leave the Harcourts' house and the party behind. Dave had humiliated her in front of her friends. And Stacy acted as if it were Tess's fault.

Fuming, she got in her car and slammed the door behind her. She wouldn't call him. She had nothing to apologize for. As she sat in the car, her feelings softened. Dave had had a bad day. He probably felt terrible already for taking it out on Tess. She had been angry with him, but she also wanted to see him, to call a truce and make up. He probably felt the same way. He might even be trying to call her already.

She jolted the car into first gear and pulled away. She wanted to make sure she was home when the phone rang.

SIXTEEN

By the time she left to meet her father for Sunday brunch, Tess still hadn't heard from Dave. She decided he had probably given up before she got home the night before, and was sleeping late after Saturday's workout. In the meantime, she had to say goodbye to her father.

They met in the lobby of the Midvale Lodge, which was famous for its extravagant brunch buffets. Her father was already there when Tess arrived. She couldn't help thinking how small he looked compared to Burt Holland, nor could she help noticing that he was nervous. He kept smoothing back his hair and pushing up his glasses as if he were with a stranger and didn't know what to say.

Neither of them said much. Tess was glad brunch was served buffet-style, since the trip to the serving table filled an empty space in the conversation. When they were seated at the table again, Tess concentrated more on her eggs and sausage and French toast than on her father.

She found she didn't know what to say, either. Cheerleading and French class seemed unimportant compared to the fact that her father was moving more than 2,000 miles away.

Not until they'd finished eating and had ordered coffee and tea did her father say, "It seems funny to be leaving Midvale, you know."

"Does it?" Tess looked up from the packet of sugar substitute she was emptying into her cup of tea. "I thought you'd be excited about moving to the West Coast. It's always been your big dream, hasn't it?"

"I guess it has. But there's something different about the reality. I'll really miss Midvale." He looked away, and for an instant Tess was struck by the sad, downward tilt of his lips. "I just thought it would be better this way. For your mother and me to live in different places."

"California seems like a pretty neat place," Tess said. "Do you think it'll be hard to find an apartment?"

Her father shook his head. "From what I've heard, there are plenty of them out there. Whatever I get, there'll always be room for you. You know that, don't you?"

"Sure, Dad. It'll be fun to visit. Everyone's going to think I'm really something, flying to L.A. for a vacation. Tess Belding, the jet-setter," she quipped.

He started asking about her schoolwork then, and about her plans to go to Winston. Tess was happy to change the subject to something more neutral. As it was she was on the verge of tears.

With an effort Tess managed to look calm, even when they were saying their farewells. "Be good to your mother, honey," her father told her as he hugged her close to him and kissed her forehead. "This isn't easy for her, I know."

"She's doing all right," Tess said over the lump that was forming in her throat.

"And you take care of yourself, too. I'll let you know as soon as I've got a place."

"Great, Dad. And have a good flight."

She stood watching as he drove off, waving until his car was out of sight. She cried all the way home.

Her mother was out when Tess, her face streaked with tears and mascara, let herself in. A note on the dining room table said, "Went to check out Handnoor's Sunday Sale. Back soon." No message that Dave had called.

Tess washed her face and redid her makeup so Alain wouldn't suspect she'd been crying. It was so summery that the cold weather on Saturday evening might have been an illusion. Tess changed into cut-off shorts and a tube top. When she checked herself in the mirror, she wondered at first if the outfit was too slinky, too revealing. Then she remembered the *Cosmo* article on French men. It said they liked women "who weren't afraid to show they were women."

"You look cool and comfortable" was Alain's first comment when she answered the door.

"I dressed for the weather," she told him.

"Yes, it is warm, isn't it?"

Alain, smiling, sat down at the dining room table, where Tess's French books were already spread out. She could swear he was looking at her with a new appreciation in his eyes as he said, "Shall we begin?"

They worked diligently. Several times Alain commented that her work seemed to have improved just since Wednesday. When her mother came home, Tess introduced her to Alain.

"My daughter has been singing your praises," Mrs. Belding told him. "She says you're an excellent teacher."

"She's an excellent student," Alain said chivalrously. "I don't see why she needs a tutor at all."

"Your friend Alain seems like a nice boy," Mrs. Belding said when Tess went upstairs after Alain had gone.

Tess nodded. "He is. He's very nice."

"But, dear—" Mrs. Belding had a note of warning in her voice.

"Hmmm?" Tess turned at the door to her room and leaned against the doorjamb.

"Well, do you think that's quite the right outfit to be wearing when you're entertaining a boy you hardly know?"

"What do you mean?"

"It's a little brief, isn't it?"

"Oh, Mom, really!" Tess rolled her eyes. "For one thing, I wasn't 'entertaining' Alain. He was tutoring me. For another, he's French, remember? He's probably used to being surrounded by girls wearing much less than this. Why, I'll bet he didn't even notice my outfit," she added, though she'd been sharply aware of Alain's eyes every now and then.

"I'm sure you're right, dear," Mrs. Belding said mildly. "But all the same, I'd be happier if you didn't wear shorts and one of those tops the next time he comes over."

Tess saluted. "Aye, aye. You're the boss," she agreed easily. But when she was inside her room, she rolled her eyes again. Who'd have thought her mother would be so old-fashioned? Obviously, her mother hadn't bothered to read the article about French men. Of course, her mother had been born and bred in the Midwest and had never visited Europe, so Tess couldn't really blame her for being so close-minded. It was probably confusing to have your own daughter end up being so much more sophisticated than you were.

That night, Tess did her nails and mended a few old pairs of jeans, listening all the time for the phone. By the time she went to bed at eleven, it still hadn't rung. She didn't even consider calling Dave. She wanted to mend things, but he was going to have to take the first step. At least she would see him the next day at school.

But she got another surprise in the morning. Dave wasn't waiting for her at her locker when she got to school, the way she'd expected him to be. When she passed him in the hall late in the morning, he was talking with Rich Stinson and Howie Fellows and gave no sign that he'd even seen her. Staring straight ahead stonily, Tess passed on.

French class was a breeze, at least. For the first time in ages, Mr. Calhoun commended her on her use of the subjunctive. But when Dave wasn't waiting for her after that class, her spirits dropped.

After school, she drove to Nicola's by herself. She wanted Dave to know that she could have a good time without him.

Dave wasn't there. But Alain Blanc was. To Tess's displeasure he was seated in a booth with Valerie Masters, Dex Grantham, and Tif Rafferty. Before Tess could join Kathy Phillips and Rich Stinson without seeming to snub her tutor, Alain waved to her, calling her name.

"Making a tour of Midvale's hot spots?" she asked brightly, but her smile was for him alone. She pointedly ignored Valerie, who was seated next to him, on the inner side of the booth.

"Valerie insists you can't be a real Midvale senior until you start hanging out at Nicola's after school," Alain told her. "So here I am."

She wanted to ask if Val had given him any

hints on being a real troublemaker, but she resisted. Valerie Masters looked smug enough already. Tess's voice was indifferent as she said, "Oh? I suppose that's true. How do you like it so far?"

"I'm not making up my mind until I taste the pizza. Dex says he gives it his highest rating—four pepperonis!"

"And we all know what a connoisseur Dex is," Tess joked, rewarding Dex with a big smile, studiously avoiding Valerie's mocking eyes.

"I can't believe Tess didn't bring you here or even take you to the mall," Valerie said in mock puzzlement. "It sounds as if she's been trying to keep you all to herself."

"Alain has been tutoring me," Tess told her coolly, "not getting a guided tour."

"That reminds me—I will have to cancel our session on Wednesday," Alain said. "I am sorry to do it so suddenly, but—well, I accepted an invitation and I am afraid it would be a great inconvenience for me to cancel."

"Sure, I understand," Tess said slowly. She didn't miss the sly look Valerie was giving Tif.

The waitress arrived with a pizza, so it was easy for Tess to make her getaway. She hurried to where Kathy and Rich were sitting and asked quickly, "Okay if I join you guys for a Coke?" She'd have preferred leaving immediately, but it would look peculiar if she walked into Nicola's and right back out again. Maybe Dave would arrive as she sat there.

Meanwhile, a question burned in Tess's mind: Was Alain calling off their lesson to spend time with Val? She couldn't imagine Alain being dishonest with her—he didn't seem the type. But Val had worn a sneaky, self-satisfied look. Val Masters obviously wasn't satisfied with trying to steal Tess's boyfriend. She wouldn't be happy until she had taken Tess's French tutor as well.

Tess found herself talking incessantly to Kathy and Rich. She wanted to forget the scene at the other table, but she also wanted to look as if she were having a fun time if Dave walked in. Once he arrived, she could take him aside and try to discuss their problems without having sacrificed her pride.

But Dave didn't come to Nicola's, and Tess finally left, sure that Rich and Kathy were relieved to get a rest from her babbling.

Dave didn't call that night, either. Of course, he might have tried to get through and given up. Mrs. Belding was on the line with Burt Holland for at least an hour. *What in the world do they have to talk about*, Tess asked herself in frustration. *They just saw each other yesterday!*

The next day at school, Dave was lounging about by her locker when Tess arrived. Reminding herself not to smile smugly, she waltzed over and spun the combination lock, ignoring him.

"Are you just going to pretend I'm not here?" he asked, moving to stand next to her.

152

"Oh, Dave!" she feigned surprise, not caring that it was transparent. "How have you been?"

"Is that all you've got to say to me?"

"Am I supposed to have something else to say?" she asked coolly.

There was a long silence. Then Dave said quietly, "No, I suppose not." And before she could tell him she was willing to listen to his apology, he stormed down the hall! Tess bit her lip as she pulled out the books she needed, then slammed the locker door. Nothing was going right, and it was all Dave's fault.

But Tess couldn't afford to concentrate only on her problem with Dave. Her French midterm was fast approaching, and she wasn't sure the progress she had made was enough to carry her through the exam. In addition, she had the new problem that Alain was obviously expanding his interests in Midvale. He had easily canceled one meeting; he could certainly do it again. If Dave was going to refuse to compromise, she would devote herself to other concerns.

When Alain agreed to come on Thursday evening for a tutoring session, Tess decided to concentrate less on verbs than on keeping her tutor's attention. Her mother worked late on Thursdays. Tess borrowed a slinky silk blouse from her mother's closet, and sprayed herself liberally with perfume from her mother's dressing table. She flirted outrageously but playfully, exactly as the magazine article had instructed, complimenting Alain on his hair, his eyes, his accent. By the end of the evening, Alain agreed to a session almost every night of the following week.

True, their sessions weren't limited to tutoring. *But,* Tess told herself, *Alain certainly deserves a little time off, and so do I, especially since Dave hasn't come to his senses.* So she took Alain out to the mall to play the computer games and to Nicola's for a slice of pizza, and she invited him over to try her famous chocolate chip cookies.

As the midterm came nearer, Tess was in such a panic when Alain wasn't there that she could barely comprehend the French words on the page in front of her. When he was there, she was so busy trying to keep him interested that she had a hard time concentrating on what he was saying. During those sessions, the reality that she might fail her midterm and lose everything that mattered came tumbling back to her. That meant cheerleading and Winston. She didn't even let herself think about Dave. She'd worry about Dave and his attitude after she'd mastered French, after she considered herself ready for the midterm.

She did try to show Dave she was ready to make up whenever he was. At the Brownville game Midvale didn't let up when they were ahead, and they trounced the opposing team 7 to 2. Dave finished the game with a total of four base-hits, two of which brought runners across home plate.

Afterward, everyone headed for Nicola's, where Tess was seated with Gina and Tony when Dave walked in. Automatically, she slid over so he could join them. But he didn't. He said hi—mostly to Gina and Tony—then stood there awkwardly for a minute.

"Good game," Tess said. "You did a great job, Dave."

"Oh?" he said. "I'm surprised you noticed."

As he walked away, Tess blinked in shock, feeling as if she'd been slapped in the face.

"What can I do?" she asked Gina and Tony. "How can he treat me this way?"

Gina shook her head in dismay. "It's not like Dave at all. How's he acted when you've tried to talk to him alone?"

"Tried to talk to him alone?" Tess sniffed. "You're making it sound as if I'm the one who's responsible for this whole frostbite treatment I'm getting! It's Dave's problem. Let him apologize."

"Maybe he doesn't know how you feel," Tony suggested.

"And maybe he doesn't think about anyone but himself," Tess retorted. Spying Alain coming in the door, she waved for him to join them. At least Alain Blanc had manners. She could live without Dave Prentice—quite happily.

SEVENTEEN

Tess's mother left early on Sunday to go into Chicago with Burt and Paul Holland to visit the Art Institute and see a musical. Tess had been invited to go with them, too, but she'd declined. She gave studying as her excuse—the midterm was coming up that Friday. But she really didn't want Paul to announce on Monday that they'd been on what could be construed as a date.

When Alain arrived, Tess was wearing her old turquoise jumpsuit and white canvas espadrilles, which she thought were very French. She dressed up the jumpsuit by leaving the top three buttons undone, adding a tight, white cinch belt, and rolling up the cuffs so her ankles showed. The heavy layer of turquoise eye shadow she wore intensified the blue of her eyes.

"*Ooh, la la!*" Alain said as he came through the door. "Aren't we sexy?"

"You like?" Tess asked, twirling around in front of him.

"Mmmm, very much," he said, his glance lingering. "It may be hard for me to concentrate on our studying this afternoon."

"Oh, Alain, what a flatterer you are," Tess said coyly. "Let me get you a nice glass of iced tea, and then we'll start."

She bounced out to the kitchen, thinking how nice it was to have a friend like Alain—one who appreciated a girl for her femininity but was an easygoing pal at the same time. *If only Dave were more like Alain*, she thought as she poured two glasses of iced tea—more carefree and not so self-absorbed.

When she went back into the other room, she was puzzled to see that Alain had taken the books from the dining room and had spread them out on the living room coffee table. "I thought we'd be more comfortable here," he said easily, looking up from where he sat on the couch.

"More comfortable—or more cozy?" Tess teased, laughing.

He smiled. "Both. Sit here"—he patted the cushion next to him—"and we'll get down to business."

She set both glasses on the table, then gingerly sat beside him. It made her kind of nervous, sitting side by side on the couch with no one else in the house. But she couldn't suggest that they go back to their usual places at the dining room table. She couldn't act like a naive little girl.

"What should we start with?" she asked, all business. "The conditional tense?" Aware that she was sitting stiffly on the edge of the couch, Tess leaned back, trying to look more casual.

He shrugged. "Whatever you like."

"All right. Let's see. *J'aimerais:* 'I would like,' as in *J'aimerais aller à Paris,* 'I would like to go to Paris.' Or, *Je voudrais:* 'I would like,' as in *Je voudrais un baiser,* 'I would like a kiss.'" She giggled.

"Would you?" he asked.

"Would I what?"

"Would you like a kiss?"

"Of course not, silly." She giggled again. "I'm conjugating verbs, remember?" She took a sip of her tea.

But as she put her glass back on the table, Alain took her forcefully in his arms and started kissing her.

It was crazy, but nice, too. In spite of herself, Tess kissed him back. It had been so long since anyone had put his arms around her, had put his lips on hers. She realized how much she really missed Dave—and yet, here was Alain, and his kisses were sweet and insistent.

But Dave's image would not leave her mind. "Alain," she murmured, gently pushing him back. "We've got to study."

"Why?" he asked, grabbing her again. "Isn't this much more enjoyable? I know what you want, Tess."

For a single kiss, she gave in. Then, as Alain's fingers searched at the buttons on her jumpsuit, she shoved him away—hard, this time. "What do you mean, you know what I want?" she gasped. "What do you think you're doing?"

"What do I think I'm doing?" he repeated, shaking his head. "What do *you* think I'm doing?"

"I think you're pawing me is what I think you're doing!" Tess told him furiously, hurling herself away from his reach. "Here I thought you were a real gentleman, but you're acting like a—a sex maniac!"

"But, Tess—" He paused, shaking his head in confusion, then smiled and reached for her again. "Ah, I see! You are playing hard to get now, eh? To make things a little spicier?"

"I am *not* playing hard to get!" she protested, jumping to her feet. Hands on her hips, she looked down at Alain, who'd collapsed, face flushed, on the couch. "I don't happen to be gettable! I *am* Dave Prentice's girl, just in case you've forgotten."

"In case *I've* forgotten!" The flush in Alain's cheeks deepened, with anger now. "I do not believe you! Lately, you are the one who's been acting as if Dave didn't exist. You've been finding excuses to get me over here, to get me to take you places. You've dressed for what were supposed to be serious sessions of studying in the flimsiest clothes imaginable! You've flirted and talked sexy and done everything to make me think you wanted me to respond to you." He snorted in disgust. "I thought American girls were supposed to be honest. How was I supposed to know you were just a tease?"

"I'm not a tease!" Tess wailed.

"If you are not a tease, what are you?" he asked evenly. "If you have not been leading me on, what in the world do you think you've been doing?"

"Studying French!" she insisted.

To her amazement, Alain laughed. "This is your idea of studying? *C'est fou!* It is plain crazy! Since the start, you've barely acted interested in French."

"I don't know what you're talking about!" Tess protested.

"No? You mean you have not worn short shorts and little tops and sweaters cut down to here for our lessons?" He jabbed himself in the chest.

She sniffed. "I didn't know being comfortable was a crime."

"You have not been flirting with me or giving me sexy looks or saying lots of things that have double meanings?"

"I've just tried to be friendly, that's all!"

"Come off it, Tess!" he exclaimed, and she couldn't help thinking that French guys sounded just like Americans when they were mad. "Every time I am near you—at Stacy's party, here, at the video arcade, anyplace—you are giving me the eye and cooing and just begging me to grab you."

"That's not true!" she protested, a bit weakly this time. "I haven't been acting like that, have I?"

He shrugged. "I do not think it is me. I do not think I've been reading things into all this that were not there."

"Maybe you're right," she admitted, the truth of Alain's accusations finally sinking in. "Oh, Alain! You must think I'm awful, and I can't say I blame you."

Alain's face was a study in puzzlement as he watched Tess sink down into a miserable heap on the floor next to the coffee table. "Maybe you should explain to me, Tess. I do not understand any of this at all."

Haltingly, Tess started at the beginning. She told him about her parents' divorce, about how terrified she was that she'd be suspended from the cheering squad and turned down at Winston, and about how much she cared for Dave and how much she missed him.

"I was so scared you'd get tired of tutoring me, I guess I started flirting to keep you around," she confessed. "And then when I read this article on French men—" In spite of her misery, she had to laugh. "I decided I had to be woman enough to keep you around."

Alain laughed, too, and the stern look on his handsome features softened. "But you're not a woman, Tess. You're a teenaged girl!"

"I know that now!" she admitted. "But I figured you were used to being surrounded by all those sexy, sophisticated Parisian girls. I was afraid you'd think I was a hick and get bored with me."

"Boring's the one thing you haven't been," Alain told her dryly. "And what makes you think the girls in Paris are so worldly? Most girls I know were brought up much more strictly than you Americans. People are actually much looser here. That is why, when you started wearing all these sexy clothes and—well, being pretty suggestive, I figured you had one thing on your mind. 'She's American,' I told myself, 'and Americans don't go in for playing games.'"

"I guess I owe you a big apology," Tess said softly. "I wouldn't blame you if you told me you'd never tutor me again. But please don't, Alain! I can't pass that midterm without your help!"

"I am going to tell you I won't be tutoring you anymore," he said slowly, and Tess felt as if her heart might stop. "But not because I'm mad at you or think you're a terrible person."

"Then why?" she wailed.

"Because you don't need me," he said simply. "And I don't think you'll let yourself believe that if I hang around. You keep telling me how dumb you are, but you're not, and I think you know that. The only reason you have any trouble with your French is because you don't concentrate enough. I know you can do it on your own."

"You're just saying that." Tess shook her head vehemently. "You want to steer clear of me because I've been such a schemer. Admit it!"

"It's not true. You just need some hard studying on your own and maybe a little help that you could get from anyone willing to quiz you on exercises in your text."

"Do you really mean that?" she asked doubtfully.

He nodded emphatically. "Definitely. As a matter of fact, I even mentioned it to Mr. Calhoun. I asked him why he thought you needed tutoring in the first place, and he told me he'd been worried about your grades because you'd done so well in the past. Don't you think maybe it's not the French itself that's bogging you down but the worrying?"

"Maybe," she agreed slowly. "But I still don't think I can do it on my own."

He got to his feet. "You'll see. All you need is faith in yourself. You can pass the midterm *and* the final without my help."

Tess wanted to beg him not to leave, but she knew that wouldn't be fair. She'd already put Alain in an awkward position. And she knew that the incident that had just taken place would hang in the air between them if they continued to study together. She had no choice but to go the last week of studying alone.

"I hope you're right," she said reluctantly. "I guess I could have studied a lot more seriously than I did. It just seems that whenever I try to concentrate on French, I get lost in daydreams."

"Just remember, all your daydreams can be reality if you pass this course with a good grade. Isn't your real life better than any fantasy?"

"I know you're right," she agreed. "I guess I'll just have to give it my best shot."

"You can do it!" he encouraged her.

They were at the door. As Alain opened it to leave, Tess asked, her voice small and hesitant, "Alain, you're not mad at me, are you?"

He smiled warmly. "Me? Of course I'm not mad at you, Tess. To tell you the truth, I think Dave Prentice is a very lucky guy."

He kissed her lightly on the lips before he walked away.

After Alain left, Tess headed straight for the phone. The time had come for her to think about Dave before it was too late. She could swallow her pride; it looked as if she'd have to, or say goodbye to Dave. She wasn't ready for that. She missed him. She was willing to be the one to make the first move.

"Hi, Tess," Mrs. Prentice said. "No, Dave's not here right now. I think he said he was going to meet some friends out at the video game arcade. He just left about half an hour ago. Shall I have him call you when he gets back?"

"That's okay, thanks, Mrs. Prentice," Tess said quickly. "I was going to take a drive out to the mall before the shops closed, anyway. I'll just peek in at the arcade." She picked up her purse and keys, buttoning her jumpsuit all the way up as she went out the door.

EIGHTEEN

The arcade was one long room lined with game machines. Tess didn't even have to go inside to see that Dave wasn't there. Howie Fellows and Dex Grantham were bent over one machine and Janet Perry and Dennis Callahan were putting quarters in another, but none of them saw her. Tess walked away, toward the center of the mall. She didn't want people to know she'd made a special trip just to look for Dave. She decided to walk down to Holton's to look at the department store's new summer clothes.

As Tess reached the end of the corridor that held the amusement arcade, she spotted Dave in the central concourse of the mall. And he was looking straight at her, with a pained expression that made her think this meeting might not go as she had planned.

Then Tess saw Valerie Masters sitting next to Dave on one of the marble benches by the central fountain. Both were holding paper cups from the pizza stand in their hands, and both were looking her way.

Well, it's now or never, Tess told herself, walking resolutely toward them. "Hi," she said, forcing a weak smile.

"Well, if it isn't Tess!" Valerie cooed. "Small world, isn't it? Or maybe I should say, small mall."

Dave didn't even speak. He just nodded.

"I called your house, and your mom said you were here." Tess ignored Valerie, looking only at Dave. Her voice was trembling and her knees were shaking. "I wanted to talk to you."

Dave stood up, and Tess was relieved that he was making it easy. Then he said, his voice level, "I can't talk now. I promised Valerie a ride home—and Dex and Howie are waiting for us to come back to the arcade."

Tess didn't dare speak or move. She was afraid her voice would break if she opened her mouth, and she knew she'd burst into tears if she looked at Val.

"Look, I'll give you a call when I get back home, okay?" Dave sighed impatiently. "Come on, Valerie, let's get back to the others."

When they were gone, Tess sank down onto the bench they'd just left. Dave was refusing to talk to her because he'd promised *Val* a ride home? How had things gotten so confused? As soon as she could trust her legs, she went back to her car. She took the long way to the parking lot, bypassing the arcade so she wouldn't have to see Dave and Valerie again.

At home, she fixed herself a tuna sandwich, then settled down to wait for Dave's call. She didn't even try to study or read or watch TV. She knew there was no chance of concentrating on French or anything else until she'd talked to Dave.

When the phone finally rang, Dave's voice at the other end of the line was soft and hesitant.

"Listen, Tess, I'm really sorry—" he began.

"It's all right, Dave," she said magnanimously. "I'm willing to forget everything. It's ridiculous for us to have been ignoring each other over something as silly as a baseball game or a party."

"Tess, that's not what I called to say I'm sorry for." Dave paused before he went on. "I was going to say I'm really sorry, but I think it's better if we don't see each other anymore."

"You what?" Her voice squeaked with shock. "You mean you're calling to break up with me? For Valerie Masters!"

"No, this has nothing to do with Valerie. It has to do with the way you've been acting—as though we've already broken up. After all, everyone in school knows there's something going on between you and Alain."

"Dave, that's absurd! You've got it all wrong!"

"I'm sick and tired of you telling me I'm

wrong about everything, Tess," he said, sounding both angry and weary. "Lately, there's been nothing I could do to make you happy. It was like I wasn't even there most of the time. All that mattered was *your* depression, *your* bad grades, *your* parents, what *you* wanted to do. I can't keep humoring you."

"Humoring me?" she retorted. "I never considered it humoring someone you loved to be concerned about what happened to them."

"I didn't, either. Not until I realized you'd gotten so used to playing the martyr there was no consoling you. Look, Tess, don't you realize everyone's getting sick and tired of your complaining all the time? So you've got to help out your mom a little more since she's started working full time—that doesn't mean you've got to keep bringing it up and making it sound as if you've been sentenced to ten years of hard labor. I want to have fun once in a while, not spend the rest of my life hearing how terrible yours is."

"Sure, you really wanted to have fun at Stacy's party!" she said smartly.

"Do you have any idea how awful I felt that night, being the one to get the losing out in the big game?" His voice was deep with emotion. "All those weeks and months of listening to your problems, of trying to tell you things were going to work out! And then one night it just so happened I could use a little sympathy, and you treat me as if I'm a big baby for feeling low, for not just grinning and bearing it or turning it into a joke. Everyone at the party that night knew I was hurting, Tess. Everyone but you. That's when I realized you'd stopped caring about me. You're too wrapped up in yourself to care about anyone else."

"That's not true, Dave!" she protested, blinking back the hot tears beginning to trickle down her cheeks. "I do care about you! I never stopped caring!"

"No?" He laughed bitterly. "Then how come you were running around all over town with Alain? I think you made it clear that you weren't sitting at home pining away over me."

"But, Dave—"

"I can't see much point in continuing this conversation," Dave said abruptly. Then, without another word, he hung up.

For a long time, Tess just stared at the receiver in her hand. Then she hung up the phone, put her head in her hands, and cried. Her good luck seemed to have run out.

Of course Dave had gotten the wrong idea about her and Alain. Alain had gotten the wrong idea himself. There was no denying it all was Tess's fault. But had she really been so self-centered lately? When she thought it over, she realized the answer was yes.

Tearfully, she phoned Gina. "Can I come over and talk to you?" she begged. "And could you call Stacy and ask her to come, too? I don't know what to do, and I need help!"

In Gina's bedroom, she told her best friends the whole story, including every embarrassing detail about what had happened with Alain and every accusation Dave had made toward her.

"Now what am I going to do?" she asked when she was through, mopping at her eyes with a sodden tissue. "Alain won't help me with my French, Dave's through with me and won't even listen to my side of the story, and I've probably lost all my friends by complaining all the time!"

"Don't get so carried away," Stacy said matter-of-factly. She put an arm around Tess and gave her a hug of consolation. "Everything's not lost yet."

"Have I really been a martyr, like Dave said?" Tess asked. "Is everyone bored with me?"

"Of course everyone's not bored with you," Stacy insisted. "Everyone at school's crazy about you. Though it is true you haven't exactly let your friends in on your life lately." She smiled sympathetically.

Tess laughed through her tears. "You've got such a diplomatic way of putting things," she said.

"What you've got to do is what I tried to get you to do a while ago," Gina said firmly. "You've got to get your life together, Tess. Sure, it's okay to feel sorry for yourself when bad things happen. But then you've got to take control and do something about it. I learned that when I was dating Dex last winter."

"But what can I do?" Tess asked. "I can't get my folks back together again."

"No," Gina admitted, "but you can start taking it for granted that you've got to help your mom out instead of feeling punished by it."

"That's not going to bring Dave back," Tess said despondently.

"No, but maybe acting like the old crazy Tess again will," Gina insisted.

"Gina's right," Stacy chimed in. "The only thing you can do now is try to show Dave you haven't really changed. Make sure you don't do anything to make him think there's really something between you and Alain, for starters."

"I don't think I have to worry about that," Tess admitted with a rueful chuckle. "Alain's probably going to be avoiding me like the plague."

"I'll bet Dave will sit up and notice when you've gone back to being the cheerful, optimistic person he was in love with," Gina said supportively.

Tess shook her head. "I still can't be very cheerful with that French midterm hanging over my head."

"We can help you study for the test," Gina insisted. "Didn't you say Alain thinks all you need is somebody to coach you straight from the textbook?"

"Do you really mean it?" Tess asked, her

heart beginning to lighten. "I could sure use you to test me when I'm through studying on my own."

"Of course we'll help," Stacy assured her. "Furthermore, I agree with Alain. There's no reason you shouldn't be able to get a handle on that course. You've just got to set your mind to it and go for it."

"I'll try!" Tess vowed. "And I promise I'll stop moping around all the time. How can I feel sorry for myself when I've got friends like you two?"

"That's more like it," Stacy said cheerfully.

They talked a while longer, then Gina said, "Why don't you two stay for supper? Dad's going to make his special Italian sausage-and-pepper heroes."

"Sounds delicious," Stacy, "but Emma's got a roast in the oven and I'm expected home."

"Tess?"

"Not me, thanks. I had a sandwich a while ago. Besides, I should try to straighten up the house a little. Mom didn't have a chance to vacuum this weekend, and it might be nice for her if she didn't come back to a mess tonight."

Gina nodded as the other two got to their feet. "I understand. And try not to worry about Valerie Masters, Tess," she added as they were leaving the room. "If she's all that's keeping Dave away from you, he'll be back in no time."

NINETEEN

Tess drove home slowly, thinking about her conversation with Stacy and Gina. She really had no right to be depressed with such good friends willing to stick by her. That thought made her start thinking about her father. She hadn't stuck by him. Her concern with her own problems had probably ruined their brunch together.

She hadn't said a single word to show him that she still loved him or that she didn't blame him for the divorce. He'd looked so fragile and unsure of himself that day. She had done nothing to let him know she understood his reasons for going to California. Tess thought of her own fantasies about Paris. It was natural that her father would have dreams of his own.

When she got home, she reread the brief note he'd written that week to say that he'd found an apartment and to give her his phone number. She dialed the phone number immediately.

"Tess!" Her father's voice brimmed with pleasure.

"Hi, Daddy. I just called to say I miss you. Could you—could you hang on while I get a tissue?"

It was a tearful, emotional conversation, but Tess was smiling by the time she hung up. She no longer doubted her father's love for her. She'd even made tentative plans to visit him before the end of summer.

When her mother came home that evening, Tess asked her frankly, "So, do you think you and Mr. Holland are going to get married?"

"Married?" Her mother's eyes widened. "Goodness, Tess, we haven't even discussed it. Don't you think it's a good idea for two people to get to know one another before they start talking about settling down?"

"But you two seem so involved," Tess insisted. "I mean, I don't want to be the last to know if you're going to be Mrs. Holland."

"Don't worry, dear," her mother assured her. "I promise you'll be the first. But I'm not in a big rush to get married again. It's hard to explain, but I feel like I'm not the same person who married your dad. It's still going to take some time for me to figure out just who I really am. And I think I'd want to have a good understanding of Beth Belding before I became Beth Holland, or Beth anyone else."

"Maybe I'm selfish, but I'm glad you're not

ready," Tess confessed. "I kind of liked having you all to myself. Now you're with Burt so much of the time, it's as if you *are* married."

"Have you been feeling left out, honey?" her mother asked with concern. "I hope not. I know you've been out of sorts lately, but—forgive me if I haven't been taking your feelings into consideration, Tess." She hesitated. "But to tell you the truth, I sort of got the idea that you didn't want to be included much."

"I know, I'm sorry. But that's going to change, if it's okay with you. I really do like Mr. Holland."

As Tess lay in bed that night, she realized that she actually did like Burt a lot. And she could tell by the way her mother's face had brightened when she'd said so that Burt Holland was making Beth Belding very happy.

I haven't been easy on Mom in other ways, either, Tess admitted to herself. Instead of sympathizing with her mother for having to work so hard at the bookstore and for being forced to give up the house she'd lived in since she was first married, Tess had groaned about a few extra chores, been rude to Burt on several occasions, and felt sorry for herself because her bedroom was a bit cramped.

She felt optimistic at school on Monday. Maybe Gina and Stacy were right. If she tried to act like her old self, everything would work out.

At least Alain hadn't given up on her

completely, in spite of the way she'd unconsciously used him. She expected him to act detached when she saw him in third-period study hall. Instead, he greeted her with a smile and a wink, then held out a piece of paper.

"What's that?" she asked, raising her eyebrows. "A warrant for my arrest?"

He laughed. "Just because we're no longer going to have tutoring sessions doesn't mean I can't give you some help. Take it. It's a passage for you to translate, using some of the problems we were working on. You can do it during study hall and I'll correct it and return it to you tomorrow."

"You're an angel!" she told him warmly. "I don't know what I've done to deserve this."

"You've been my first real friend in America," he answered simply. "Isn't that enough?"

As she worked through the few paragraphs written in Alain's small, neat handwriting, she found herself smiling. Alain had written the passage to show Tess he wasn't angry with her: it was about friendship, misunderstandings, and the importance of honesty.

"Here you are," she said, handing her English translation to Alain as the bell rang to announce the end of the period. "Believe it or not, I didn't have too much trouble. Maybe I've actually learned something."

"I know you can pass this test," he said as they walked from the room together.

She grinned ruefully. "To tell the truth, I didn't have a whole lot of anything else to do besides study."

"Don't worry, Tess. Something tells me things will work out with you and Dave," he assured her, putting his arm around her shoulders and giving her a friendly squeeze.

At the same moment Dave came striding down the corridor in their direction. He took one look at Tess standing there with Alain's arm encircling her shoulders, and his pleasant smile vanished. He glared at her, his eyes dark with contempt, then stormed past without acknowledging the presence of either of them.

"Whoops!" Alain murmured with a grimace. "I'm not helping your cause any, am I?"

"Don't worry," she assured him. "I don't expect it to be easy. I almost feel as if I deserve to have Dave snub me."

When she thought back over the last few weeks, she couldn't blame Dave for losing patience with her. He'd tried to cajole her into relaxing and having a good time, but she'd preferred pouting and forcing him to coddle her. Then she'd done everything she could to give him the impression that she was romantically involved with Alain. She'd created a very complicated situation for herself. She couldn't expect it to disappear overnight.

For once, she was almost glad French was such a grind for her. Studying intensely every night of the week helped keep her mind off

Dave. When she did start missing him—so much she could have cried—she just memorized French instead. It was impossible to think of anything else but the language when she was quizzing herself by closing the textbook and writing down irregular verbs from memory, reciting conjugations in her mind from morning to night. Only when she'd turned out the light and crawled under the covers did the depth of her loss sweep over her. It was hard for her to imagine a life without Dave, so sleep came easily to her: in her dreams, he was always there.

On Wednesday afternoon, she saw Dave coming toward her in the hall. She steeled herself to give him a smile and a soft "hi." She was terrified he'd pretend she wasn't there. But he relented and gave her a nod. It wasn't much, but it *was* progress.

When Paul Holland stopped by her locker after school that day, Tess found herself deep in conversation with him before she even realized she didn't find him annoying for a change.

"Wouldn't it be neat if your mom and my dad got serious about each other?" he asked. "You know, really serious? I can't think of anything I want more than to have a real family again. I mean, Dad's always been great, but it's not the same just having one parent, is it? You know, I can still remember weird things from when Mom was alive: how the kitchen used to smell when she was baking and the way she always lit the candles for dinner even if it was

179

just us three. I'll bet your mom would be neat to live with."

Tess couldn't say anything. She felt too sad to speak. She'd never thought much about how lonely it must have been for Paul, growing up without a mother. Paul obviously thought his father was great. But he was a busy man with a demanding business to run. It wasn't surprising that Paul had ended up a bit lost or that he wanted so desperately to be liked and accepted that he sometimes overdid it.

Finally, taking a deep breath, she told him, "Yep, she's a pretty neat mother. I'm not sure *I'm* so neat to live with, though," she added, laughing shakily.

"Come on, I'll bet that's not true," he insisted. "Hey, I can't think of anybody in all of Midvale I'd rather have as a sister. I've always felt that way," he went on shyly, not looking at her. "I can't tell you how excited I was when I found out my dad was going out with your mom. I kept thinking, wow, Tess Belding's mom is dating my dad, and that means I'm going to get to visit my favorite cheerleader at home!"

"Stop complimenting me so much, Paul!" she scolded with a smile. "You're spoiling me." *He really does idolize me*, she realized. He'd never been trying to gain popularity at her expense. He'd never been anything but genuinely friendly to her, in spite of the way she continually snubbed him. Other kids had always liked him—like Sherri Callahan, who was secure enough not to worry about whether or not the other kids approved of Paul.

Dave was right about Paul, Tess thought as she headed home from school. If only Dave would give her a chance to let him know she finally understood how right he'd been about her behavior toward Burt's son.

The day before midterms, Tess came out of French class and almost collided with Dave at the water fountain. "Ooops!" she blurted nervously. "Good old Tess, never looking where she's going!"

"How are you doing?" he asked, with a smile that bore a touch of their old closeness and tore at her heart. *How did I ever let him slip away so carelessly*, she wondered. *I'll never find a boy like Dave again.*

Swallowing hard, she answered, "Not bad, thanks."

"How are things at home?" he said softly.

"Pretty good. Do you know, I really think Mom and Mr. Holland could end up getting married?"

He looked puzzled. "How come you sound so happy about it? I thought having Paul Holland as a stepbrother was a fate worse than death?"

"Oh, Paul's not so bad," she admitted, seizing the opportunity to let Dave know how she felt. "To tell the truth, now that I've gotten to know him better, I actually like him."

"He's a good guy," Dave agreed. "All ready for midterms?"

She made a face. "As ready as I'll ever be, I suppose. My French test's tomorrow, but I think I may actually pass."

"Good luck," he said over the ringing of the bell. He clasped her shoulder lightly before he turned and hurried off.

Tess blinked away the tears welling up in her eyes. She couldn't start feeling weepy about Dave—not with less than twenty-four hours to go before her French midterm.

Gina and Stacy had gotten permission to spend the night at Tess's so they could help her with last-minute cramming. Both proved to be tireless tutors. They stayed up until one in the morning, bleary-eyed and hoarse, until Tess was perfect on every exercise. Then the three of them toppled into bed—Stacy and Gina in the twin beds in Tess's room, Tess creeping into the other side of the king-sized bed in her mother's room—and went right to sleep.

Both girls were waiting by Tess's locker after French class the next day. "How did it go?" Gina asked anxiously, her eyes puffy from lack of sleep.

"Good news or bad news?" Stacy asked with a sleepy yawn.

"I'll know on Tuesday when the grades are posted," Tess answered simply. "I don't even want to think about it till then. But I *seemed* to know what I was doing."

Both of them exhaled loudly. "We'll just have to keep our fingers crossed," Gina said.

Even though it was over, the French exam was all Tess could think about during the weekend. Her cheering certainly suffered for it, though Midvale managed to win their ball game without Tess's wholehearted assistance. She couldn't keep from remembering the test questions she hadn't been definite about.

The morning the midterm results would be posted in the corridor by the auditorium, Tess was almost late to school. She was dying to see how she'd done, but she was scared, too, and the scared part of her kept finding reasons to delay leaving the house.

When she did approach the bulletin board in the hallway, Gina and Stacy were already there.

"How'd I do?" she asked nervously, her stomach churning at their tense expressions.

"We haven't found Calhoun's grades yet," Stacy said impatiently. "There're so many other results here. I got an A in English."

"Well, that's good. Maybe that's a sign," Tess said, trying to be optimistic as her eyes rapidly scanned the papers tacked to the board. "Here it is: Mr. Calhoun, Fourth-Year French Midterm Grades."

"Let's see." Gina craned her neck, but Tess saw the big letter by her name first.

"Yahoo!" She let out a loud yell and jumped

up in the air. "Look at that! A B−, even better than I thought I could possibly do!"

"You're on the squad!" Gina yelled triumphantly.

"You're into Winston!" Stacy joined in.

"I did it! I did it! And I never could have without the two of you!" Tess threw her arms around her friends, momentarily forgetting she was clutching her schoolbooks, which soared into the air and then skittered across the floor.

As she looked to where they'd landed, Tess was mortified to see that they'd skidded to a stop at the feet of Valerie Masters, who was walking down the hall with Dave.

Valerie was smirking and rolling her eyes at Dave. But Dave couldn't have seen Val's mocking expression because he was already squatting down to retrieve Tess's books.

"Come on, Dave," Valerie snapped as he crossed the corridor, the books clutched in his hands. "We'll be late for homeroom."

"Go ahead," Dave called back over his shoulder. "I'll get there before the last bell."

Tess stared wordlessly as Valerie stalked off, glaring. Behind her she could feel Stacy and Gina fading away as the first bell reverberated through the halls.

"Sorry about that," Tess murmured, holding out her hand to take the books. "I guess I got carried away."

"You look like you've got something to celebrate," Dave said warmly. He nodded toward the posted papers. "How'd you do in French?"

"A B−," Tess told him happily. "Not the best grade in the world, but good enough to keep me on the cheering squad and get me into Winston. I not only passed, I raised my grade average, and that's what counts."

"See?" Dave said. "I always told you you could do it."

"Too bad I had to make such a mess of my life before I believed you," Tess said lightly. "Why didn't you ever tell me what an idiot I was acting like?" Then she caught her breath as it hit her that she and Dave were alone—and that he'd sent Valerie on her way.

Dave didn't say anything for a few moments. He just stood there, gazing down at Tess, who couldn't tear her eyes away from him. She felt as if she wanted to memorize every feature of his face, every wave in his thatch of sandy hair. Finally, he said softly, "Come on, I'll walk you to homeroom."

"I'm still a little weak in the knees from seeing my grade," Tess told him, walking slowly so she could spend extra seconds in his company.

"You must have really worked, Tess. I'm proud of you."

"I've got a real grasp of the language now, I think. And I like it better now that I know what I'm doing." *I like being so close to you again, too*, she wanted to say. But she knew she'd have to take it slowly. She was willing to take some time to prove to Dave that he could trust her again.

"By the way," she said as they walked along, ignoring the clanging of the second bell, "I think I've owed you an apology for a long, long time . . ."